Escape
F Car   39092000392169

Silver City Public Library

ESCAPE

The Earl of Kyleston runs away from London to Paris to escape the attentions of a beautiful woman who is determined to marry him.

In Paris a young woman calls on him who is obviously suffering from acute malnutrition and although her clothes are almost threadbare, he realises she is a lady. She goes to him in desperation because her mother is dying and she asks him to help her, saying the only way she could possibly earn enough money, as she would not accept charity, was to become a *demi-mondaine*.

The Earl, who had never heard such an extraordinary request in his life, is astonished, and while he lends Miranda the money it takes a short while before he discovers she is actually a relation.

Her mother dies and while he is wondering how he can help her he is busily engaged in enquiring into the very intricate situation between the French and the Germans.

Paris is also in a riotous, disruptive state and when the Earl is taking Miranda to the Opera he is knocked down by a brick thrown by the rioters.

While he is unconscious the siege of Paris begins and there seems no escape for the Earl and Miranda.

How this exciting situation is solved is told in this 375th book by Barbara Cartland.

ABOUT THE AUTHOR

Barbara Cartland, the world's most famous romantic novelist, who is also an historian, playwright, lecturer, political speaker and television personality, has now written over 370 books and sold over 370 million over the world.

She has also had many historical works published and has written four autobiographies as well as the biographies of her mother and that of her brother, Ronald Cartland, who was the first Member of Parliament to be killed in the last war. This book has a preface by Sir Winston Churchill and has just been republished with an introduction by Sir Arthur Bryant.

"*Love at the Helm*", a recent novel, was written with the help and inspiration of the late Admiral of the Fleet, the Earl Mountbatten of Burma. This is being sold for the Mountbatten Memorial Trust.

Miss Cartland in 1978 sang an Album of Love Songs with the Royal Philharmonic Orchestra.

In 1976 by writing twenty-one books, she broke the world record and has continued for the following seven years with 24, 20, 23, 24, 24, 25 and 22. In the "Guinness Book of Records" she is listed as the world's top-selling author.

In private life Barbara Cartland, who is a Dame of Grace of the Order of St. John of Jerusalem, Chairman of the St. John Council in Hertfordshire and Deputy President of the St. John Ambulance Brigade, has fought for better conditions and salaries for Midwives and Nurses.

She has championed the cause for old people, had the law altered regarding gypsies and founded the first Romany Gypsy camp in the world.

Barbara Cartland is deeply interested in Vitamin therapy, and is President of the National Association for Health.

Her designs "Decorating with Love" are being sold all over the U.S.A. and the National Home Fashions League made her, in 1981, "Woman of Achievement".

"Barbara Cartland's Romances" (Book of Cartoons) has been published in Great Britain, and the U.S.A.

In 1984, she received at Kennedy Airport in America the Bishop Wright Air Industry Award for her contribution to the development of aviation, when in 1931 she and two RAF officers thought of, and carried, the first aeroplane-towed glider Airmail

ESCAPE

ESCAPE

Barbara Cartland

SEVERN HOUSE PUBLISHERS

This first U.S.A. hardcover edition published 1989 by
SEVERN HOUSE PUBLISHERS INC., New York.
First world edition published 1985 by
SEVERN HOUSE PUBLISHERS LTD., of
40–42 William IV Street, London WC2N 4DF

Copyright © Barbara Cartland, 1985

British Library Cataloguing in Publication Data
Cartland, Barbara
Escape.
I. Title
823'.912 [F]   PR6005.A765
ISBN 0-7278-1223-8

Distributed in the U.S.A. by
Mercedes Distribution Center, Inc.
62 Imlay Street, Brooklyn, New York 11231

All rights reserved. Unauthorised duplication contravenes
applicable laws.

Printed and bound in Great Britain

AUTHOR'S NOTE

The Siege of Paris lasted 130 days. The suffering had been intense from the bombardment, smallpox, typhoid and, of course, lack of food.

By mid-January bread was rationed to just over half-a-pound a day and half this amount for children under five, although its quality was bad enough to cause many infant deaths from enteritis. Meat, when there was any, was a quarter-of-a-pound a week for adults.

Paris was also gripped by the bitterest winter in living memory and every tree and fence was torn down for fuel.

On November 12th the shrewd, level-headed American Minister, Elihu Washburne wrote:

"Fresh meat is getting almost out of the question. ... They have begun on dogs, cats and rats. ... The gas is also giving out."

One of the first to try the new fare was Henry Labouchere, and what I have written about him in this novel is factual.

As early as 1791 the French were using balloons for military purposes. During the Siege after September 23rd when Durouf had made his successful solo flight to Evieux, the Minister of Posts decreed the establishment of a "Balloon Post" and balloons took off at a rate of two or three a week.

By a miracle until November 28th, and the 34th balloon, there was not a single fatality.

Altogether, 65 manned balloons left Paris during the Siege. They carried 164 passengers, 381 pigeons, five dogs and nearly 11 tons of official despatches, including 2,500,000 letters. Only five fell into enemy hands.

Blanche d'Antigny, 1840–1874, was the nicest of the *Grandes Horizontales*. What I have written about her is true and she did turn part of her "*hôtel*" into a hospital and looked after the wounded herself.

Two years after the war a journalist records that Breton soldiers had not forgotten their "good little sister of Charity" as they called her, and often sent her chickens, pigeons and potatoes.

CHAPTER ONE
1870

The Earl of Kyleston walked through the impressive entrance of the finely built house in the Champs Elysées and said to a servant as he did so:

"Has *Monsieur le Vicomte* returned?"

"*Non, Monsieur.*"

The Earl walked into a comfortable Salon on the ground floor and almost immediately a flunkey appeared with champagne and a plate of *pâté* sandwiches.

He looked at them somewhat indifferently as if he

was not hungry and put down the glass of champagne without tasting it on a small table beside his chair.

Then as he sat back he told himself he was bored – bored with the audience he had just had with the French Minister, bored with the luncheon which had seemed interminable at the British Embassy, bored although it seemed incredible, even with the alluring *horizontale* with whom he had spent most of the night.

At thirty-three the Earl was considerably *blasé* and, as his relatives often said behind his back, spoilt.

Everything had been too easy for him from the moment he was born, and the fact that when he was twenty-two he had inherited his father's title, the huge estates, and the great wealth that went with it, had made life a bed of roses where he was concerned.

He was, in fact, a considerable personality in his own right and, being extremely athletic, excelled at every sport in which he was interested.

Most of all, he was a magnificent rider, while his race-horses were first past the winning-post in the Classic races very much more often than those of his rival owners.

Although the Earl would give his whole mind, his time, and his attention to his horses and his other animals, and there was no detail on his estates or his houses that was too small to receive his consideration, he grew quickly impatient with people.

Where women were concerned, his love-affairs never lasted very long.

It was in fact the evaporation of a love-affair which brought him now from England to Paris.

He had pursued Lady Irene Curtis with an ardour which surprised even himself.

She was certainly exremely beautiful and had glowed

like a star in the Social firmament when she arrived unexpectedly in the middle of the London Season.

Every man who saw her was immediately bowled over by her loveliness, but when the Earl had swept them all to one side it was not surprising that Lady Irene had succumbed to his persuasions even more quickly than he had dared to anticipate.

Then when she was within his grasp, astonishingly and most unexpectedly he found that she no longer excited him.

It was impossible to diagnose in what respect she failed him or why anyone as beautiful as Lady Irene should suddenly cease to attract him.

But after a very short period of being her acknowledged lover, he knew he had to escape.

Because they had been so talked about and the whole of the Social World was expecting them to announce their engagement, the Earl knew that it was going to be more difficult to extract himself from this particular situation than it had been from similar entanglements in the past.

The difference now was that Lady Irene was of great Social consequence and she was determined, almost as fiercely as a tigress at bay, that the Earl should not escape.

The daughter of the Duke of Cumbria, she had been married when she was eighteen to a wealthy young Peer with whom she had little in common.

His protestations of undying love were not substantiated by his actions and, being infatuated with the stage, he soon returned to the actresses whose bawdy exuberance was far more to his liking than the ladylike behaviour of his well-bred wife.

Lady Irene was not particularly distressed, as she

had found after her marriage, even while living quietly in the country, there were a great number of men only too willing to pay her court.

It was, however, only after her husband's sudden death in an accident and the subsequent year of mourning that she had come to London and realised she was able to captivate the most sophisticated and critical Society in the whole of Europe.

After the strict propriety of the Prince Consort which had made the Court at Buckingham Palace extremely dull, London had begun to burst out into a new era of pleasure-seeking enjoyment.

The Prince of Wales quite openly disclosed that every pretty woman he saw attracted him, and his lead was gladly followed by the majority of the aristocracy.

Lady Irene realised almost immediately that she had a wide choice and, having once set eyes on the Earl of Kyleston, she knew she need look no further.

Never had she imagined a man could be so handsome, so raffish and so exceedingly masculine.

She was mad about Thornton Kyleston, and it had seemed as if he felt the same way about her, until quite suddenly, almost as if he had fallen down to earth from one of the newfangled and much-talked-about balloons, the Earl was bored.

"I must get away," he told himself, but he knew it was going to be difficult.

The one thing he really disliked was recriminations, reproaches, and the unanswerable question: "Why do you not love me any more?"

He was, however, extremely dexterous in getting himself out of a hole, and a visit to the Foreign Secretary provided him with exactly the excuse he needed to go to Paris.

"To tell you the truth, Kyleston," Lord Granville had said, "I am finding it very difficult from the conflicting reports I receive, to know exactly what is going on. You have helped the Foreign Office before, and I should be extremely grateful if you would help us again."

"I will certainly do my best," the Earl replied, "but I should have thought it was pretty obvious that the Germans intend business, while the French, as usual, are being frivolous about it."

"You may be right," Lord Granville agreed. "At the same time, knowing your shrewdness in matters like this, I shall wait eagerly to hear what you have to tell me."

He paused before he added:

"Use the usual code and make sure that any messenger you send with your letters is not apprehended."

"I will take every precaution," the Earl promised, then added:

"What is our Ambassador doing?"

"Shall I say Lord Lyon is not as communicative as I would wish," the Foreign Secretary replied with a smile.

"Then I will certainly try not to disappoint you," the Earl laughed.

Lady Irene was shattered at the news of his departure for France.

"Darling Thornton, how can you contemplate for a moment deserting me when we are so happy and when there are so many marvellous Balls to attend?"

The Earl, who disliked Balls, managed to reply in what sounded quite a sincere tone:

"You can hardly imagine it is something I positively wish to do, but there are reasons which I cannot explain, but which concern our country, which make it imperative for me to visit Paris."

Lady Irene's eyes had widened with surprise.

"Are you telling me you are in the Secret Service, or something like that?" she asked.

"Certainly not!" the Earl said sharply, knowing what a chatterbox she was. "But I do happen to have many friends in Ministerial posts in France and, as you know, the political situation there appears to be in somewhat of a mess."

He knew as he spoke that Lady Irene had not the slightest idea of it, and if she had was not interested.

But he realised with some relief that he had impressed her, and she therefore did not make as much fuss about his leaving as he had feared.

"Come back quickly, dearest!" she said. "I shall be desperately lonely without you, and shall miss your kisses every hour and every minute of every day."

The Earl thought cynically there was no likelihood of her being lonely.

At the same time he realised that, if she had a heart, she was prepared to give it into his keeping, and although it was tiresome he might have to stay in Paris for longer than he intended.

He knew however that Paris was at the moment the gayest City in the world, and there would be a profusion of beautiful women, only too willing to save him from feeling lonely, either by day or by night.

When he arrived in Paris he went straight to stay with an old friend, the *Vicomte* de Soissons, who was always delighted to have him, and this at least rescued him from having to stay at the British Embassy which he would have found intolerably boring.

The *Vicomte*, who was a few years older than

himself, managed with the dexterity of the French to have a charming wife whom he left in the country with his children.

He himself lived in Paris where he was a leading light in the brilliant, witty and wildly extravagant Social Set which circled round the Prince Napoleon.

At the Prince's parties the Earl knew he would find the most outrageous and expensive of the dazzling *demi-mondaines* who were so experienced in entertaining a man that it was impossible for him to have even a moment's boredom in their company.

The dinner-party last night, the Earl thought, had certainly been amusing, and as there were several distinguished Ministers present, he had learnt quite a lot which he intended to pass on to Lord Granville by secret code.

He found himself quite entranced by his partner at dinner whose dark, flashing eyes and jet black hair, and her skill in giving everything she said a *double entendre* made her different in every way from Lady Irene.

Yet, strangely enough, when he left her house as dawn was breaking over the grey roofs of Paris, he found himself yawning, not because he was tired, but because he was thinking that the night had a certain lack of novelty about it.

It was almost as if, he thought, he was reading a chapter of a book he had already read before.

"What do I want?" he asked himself. "What the devil is the matter with me?"

Because he was very intelligent he knew the answer.

It was that he did not have to exert himself enough, and was using only a small fraction of his considerable brain power in his daily approach to life.

Once long ago he had toyed with the idea of

entering the Foreign Office, but he knew that he did not wish to be tied to a desk, nor did he really think the strange behaviour of other nations was anything to do with him.

"I suppose if I had to take part in a war," he thought, "I would be so concerned with keeping myself alive that I would not have time to ask if I enjoyed or was interested in what I was doing."

Such speculation however was no satisfactory answer to his personal problem.

He therefore picked up his glass of champagne and thought wistfully that men who drowned their troubles in drink had more good sense than people gave them credit for.

"Perhaps I should go exploring," he told himself. "A life of adventure would certainly be better than listening to the tedious nonsense I have had to endure at luncheon today."

He took another sip of his champagne and at that moment the door opened.

He looked round eagerly, hoping his friend the *Vicomte* had returned, but instead a servant came into the room to say in French:

"There is a lady here, *Monsieur*, who has asked if she can see you."

"A lady?" the Earl enquired, wondering if his partner of the night before had decided to pursue him or, which seemed even more improbable, that Lady Irene had followed him to Paris.

"It is a young woman, *Monsieur*," the servant went on. "She appears to be in some distress."

Now the Earl was surprised and, because there seemed to be no good reason to turn her away, he said:

"Show her in, but make it clear that I cannot give her more than a few minutes."

The servant, who had been with the *Vicomte* for many years, understood.

He went from the room with a knowing look in his eyes.

The Earl rose to his feet to stand looking very tall and authoritative with his back to the mantelpiece.

As the door opened again to admit a young woman he saw at a glance that she was obviously a Lady, but at the same time extremely poor.

The Earl was very observant and he was also very shrewd in appreciating and understanding another person's character.

He had trained himself, because he found it interesting, to watch for every flicker of an eye-lid, the twist of a lip, or a nervous movement that would tell him what a man or woman was thinking or feeling.

He believed he had taught himself so well that it would be impossible for anybody, however astute, to lie to him without his being aware of it.

The woman who advanced towards him was, he realised, extremely pretty but in an unusual manner.

He could not explain this until when she was standing in front of him he realised she was too thin for it to be natural, and the bones of her wrists were protruding in a way which was a sign of malnutrition.

She was neatly dressed in good taste, but he could see her gown was almost threadbare and the jacket she wore over it was faded and obviously thin with age.

She had fair hair and her eyes, which seemed enormous owing to the excessive thinness of her face, were grey. They held at the moment, to the Earl's surprise, an unmistakable expression of fear.

She dropped him a small curtsy with a grace that he appreciated, then said in a soft, melodious voice:

"I am very grateful to Your Lordship for agreeing to see me."

"You are English!" the Earl exclaimed.

"My father was English, which is why I have .. come to you."

"As you seem to know who I am," the Earl said, "perhaps you would tell me your name."

"It is Miranda .. Valmont," she replied.

The Earl thought it strange that if her father was English she should have a French surname, but as if she knew what he was thinking she explained:

"As I live in Paris I use my mother's name, who is French."

The Earl smiled.

"Will you sit down, Miss Valmont, or *Mademoiselle* if you prefer, and tell me what I can do for you."

The girl, for he realised she was quite young, did as he said, twisting her fingers together rather nervously.

He thought that perhaps because he was standing up and was so tall he was intimidating her.

He therefore sat down in a chair beside her and said in a tone which most women found irresistible:

"Tell me what is your trouble."

She looked away from him and after a moment she said in a low voice:

"It .. seemed easy .. when I saw in the .. newspaper that you had .. arrived in Paris .. to ask for your assistance .. but now .. I am afraid you .. will not understand."

"Shall I say that whatever you have to tell me I will be as understanding and sympathetic as I can?"

"That is .. very kind of you."

The Earl smiled.

"How can you be sure of that until you have told me what you want? Do you live in Paris?"

"My mother and I have been living here for five years, since my .. f .. father died."

She spoke quickly as if it was important for him to understand. Then she said:

"For the last year my mother has been .. ill .. very ill and .. now the Doctors say she must undergo an operation. If she does not do so .. she will .. die!"

"I am sorry," the Earl said quietly.

There was silence until he continued with a note of cynicism in his voice that he could not suppress:

"I presume, Miss Valmont, that you are asking me if I will give you the money to save your mother's life."

He thought as he spoke that, compared with the innumerable people who had begged from him in one way or another during the year, this was quite a new approach and at least this girl, or someone for her, had thought out something more original.

But then to his surprise Miranda gave a little cry of horror and said:

"No, no, of course not! I would not think of begging! My mother and I have our .. pride!"

The Earl glanced down at her wrists and said gently:

"And yet you are starving!"

"How do you know .. how did you guess?" Miranda asked in surprise.

"Shall I say I am very observant," the Earl answered, "and I can see you are extremely under-nourished and much too thin for someone of your age."

There was silence, then she gave what was almost a sob before she said:

"Y .. you are .. right .. and Mama needs milk, eggs

and chicken which we cannot afford in order to give her strength for the .. operation which is a .. very serious one."

Before the Earl could speak she added:

"But I am not asking for money .. I would rather die than do that .. and so would Mama!"

The Earl was puzzled.

"Then what are you asking?"

To his surprise the colour rose in Miranda's cheeks, sweeping up from her chin to her eyes and making her look unexpectedly lovely.

The Earl was waiting and after a moment she said hesitatingly:

"As I live in Paris .. you will understand that I have often seen the .. beautiful women whom Dumas described as the *'demi-mondaines'*."

The Earl raised his eye-brows, but he did not interrupt and Miranda went on:

"The newspapers write of the jewels they have been given .. the horses they drive .. the treasures that .. ornament their houses and, of course, the .. extravagance of the .. parties which take .. place in them."

She spoke in a soft, hesitating but at the same time musical, voice which the Earl found himself listening to, not only with surprise at what she was saying, but also at the way she said it.

Then her colour deepened and he knew it was impossible for her to look at him as she said:

"Please .. can you tell me how I can .. become one of these .. women and make enough .. money .. for Mama's operation and for .. food that will help to .. make her strong and .. well."

The Earl for a moment could hardly believe what she had said.

Then he thought it was the strangest thing he had ever been asked in his life.

He could however understand her reasoning: she obviously thought it was the only way she could possibly make enough money and that it could seem to her easy in Paris where the *grandes horizontales*, adept in the *sciences galantes* were the centre of attraction.

Because he was silent Miranda said quickly:

"I .. I know you are .. shocked .. I know it is wrong of me to .. suggest anything so .. wicked .. but I have thought and thought .. and there seems nothing else I can do."

She turned to look at him and say beseechingly:

"I would .. scrub floors .. I would do anything to help Mama .. but I cannot leave her alone for long .. and I must have the money for the operation .. quickly."

"I understand," the Earl said seriously, "but as I think your idea, Miss Valmont, is very impractical, you must allow me to think of some other way of finding the money that will save your mother."

Miranda gave a little cry and she said:

"I know you will think it wrong of me .. but please do not .. insult me by offering me the money unless I can give you .. something in return."

As if she felt he was unimpressed she said, and now her eyes flickered and he knew she was very shy:

"I .. have been told .. there are .. men .. who prefer very young women who are .. innocent and .. untouched. Surely you must know of someone .. like that?"

The Earl knew exactly what she was saying, and because he found it so extraordinary he rose to his feet to walk across the room and stand at the window looking out at the small garden that surrounded the house.

He was thinking that never in his life had anybody brought him such a strange problem, or one which he realised he had to handle with even more tact and diplomacy than he would expend on the investigations he was undertaking on behalf of Lord Granville.

Because he was very perceptive, he was aware that if he insisted bluntly on paying for the operation, as he was indeed quite ready to do, there was every likelihood that Miranda with her sense of pride would leave immediately.

He would then be unable to find her, having no idea of where she lived.

Perhaps, he thought for a moment, that was the simplest solution to the problem. But he knew it was because he was English that she had come to him.

He was well known as a sportsman and he knew he could not leave this child to cope with her own difficulties when it was quite obvious she was incapable of doing so.

Without turning round he was aware that Miranda's eyes were on him, her fingers clasped fervently together, and he had an idea that she was praying.

He turned from the window and walked back to sit down once again in the chair beside her.

"I have been thinking about your problem, Miss Valmont," he said, "and I presume your mother has seen a reputable Doctor?"

"Yes," Miranda replied. "He is young, so he is not very well known, but he is extremely intelligent, and I know that he is not lying to me when he says that only an operation can save Mama .. and then only if it is done .. quickly!"

"And he has suggested that he should do it?" the Earl asked, thinking that perhaps a young Doctor, of whom he was suspicious, might just be exploiting a rather ignorant girl.

"No, of course not," Miranda answered. "He brought a Surgeon to see Mama, who would do the operation privately. He is a very experienced man. I checked as much as I could on his credentials and found he has, in fact, operated on a great number of important Frenchmen and their wives."

"I see you have been very sensible," the Earl said. "Now, how much is this operation going to cost?"

Miranda drew in her breath. Then she named a sum in francs which the Earl quickly calculated as being a little over a hundred pounds.

"It is a .. great deal of money, My Lord," Miranda said nervously, "but I could not allow Mama to enter an ordinary hospital, where I am told they butcher the patients and the building itself is not clean. Often patients catch there a far worse disease than the one they went in with!"

It was what the Earl already knew, and he nodded.

Then as she knew he was thinking, Miranda bent towards him, her hands clasped together.

"Please .. please .. help me," she begged. "There is no other .. way by which I can .. save Mama, and she is already very weak from lack of food."

"As you are," the Earl said.

As if it was a thought that had suddenly occurred to him, he went to the table on which the servant had placed the *pâté* sandwiches and the champagne.

He picked up the plate and taking it over to Miranda said:

"While we are thinking, and we have to think this

over very carefully, I suggest you have a sandwich. I was just about to eat one myself when you arrived."

He saw by the sudden glint in her eyes how hungry she was, and yet for a moment she hesitated and he had the feeling she was about to refuse.

Then slowly her hand with its bone-like fingers went out to take a sandwich and as she lifted it to her lips the Earl was aware that she was controlling herself to be slow, because it would have seemed vulgar to gobble it down.

He put the plate down beside her on the little table and returned to the grog-tray to fetch her half a glass of champagne, at the same time filling his own glass, and said:

"Now as we have to be very sensible about this, Miss Valmont, I think a little champagne will help our brains to work better."

She did not say anything, but he knew she was afraid to drink it because she had had so little to eat that it might make her dizzy.

He sipped from his own glass, then he said:

"I suppose you understand what these ladies you describe as *demi-mondaines* do to earn their money?"

Again Miranda blushed before, in a very small voice, she said:

"I think they allow the .. gentlemen make .. love to them and because the women make them happy .. they give them in return .. beautiful jewels .. and also .. money."

"And you think that is what you could do?" the Earl asked somewhat sarcastically.

There was a little pause. Then Miranda said:

"I think, My lord .. you are telling me that I .. would be a failure and perhaps any gentleman to whom you .. introduced me would be .. angry and refuse to .. pay me."

She spoke so wistfully, and seemed so pathetic, that the Earl said quickly:

"No, I was thinking nothing of the sort. I was merely trying to make you realise that as a Lady, which I can see you undoubtedly are, you would find it very hard to emulate the Courtesans of whom you have heard so much, and who are of a very different class to yourself."

He paused, then continued:

"Many of them have more by good fortune than anything else, reached the position in which they find themselves. What we are talking about is the few who have made it what you might call a very profitable profession. There are hundreds, if not thousands, of women who have attempted to emulate them, and failed."

"I .. I understand what you are .. saying to me," Miranda replied, "but .. if I cannot earn money that way .. then what else can I do?"

There was a note of desperation in her voice and the Earl said:

"Now listen to me, Miss Valmont. I want you to be sensible. You are English and so am I, and I think, because we are both in a foreign country, that there is not only a bond between us, but we also have to help one another."

At his words, Miranda looked up at him, and he saw that now the worried expression in her eyes had disappeared and had been replaced by one of hope.

"What I am going to suggest," the Earl went on, " is that I lend you the money for your mother's operation, and it will definitely be a loan and not a gift. And because I am certain you would like me to be businesslike about it, you shall pay me interest on the loan at a small percentage which will be payable as soon as it is convenient for you to do so, but not while it means unnecessary hardship for you."

He knew that Miranda was listening intently, trying to understand exactly what he was saying, and after a moment she said almost childishly:

"That would .. not be the same as .. giving it to me?"

"Certainly not!" the Earl said. "You will sign a document saying what you owe me, and from time to time – shall we say every six months? – you will inform me of your address and what position you are in. By that means I can keep a watch on my money and not be afraid of losing it altogether."

He spoke briskly and in a businesslike way, and he knew that Miranda was turning over in her mind whether he was helping her simply out of charity.

Her pride would not have allowed that, but she knew that he was giving her a chance of saving her mother in a way she had never expected.

The Earl rose and walked to the desk which was on the other side of the room.

"I am going to make out a note of indemnity which you will sign," he said, "and because I think it is going to be difficult for you to repay it at all quickly, the interest on the loan will be only two percent."

"I am afraid I .. know nothing about .. such matters," Miranda said, "although I feel sure that is much too low."

"If I am to be a usurer," the Earl said with a smile, "it is not for you to complain!"

"I .. I am not complaining," Miranda said quickly,

"indeed I am very .. very grateful .. more than I can possibly say. I am sure it is .. wrong of me to accept such kindness .. and I swear to you I did not .. come here .. expecting you to help me .. like this."

The Earl knew she was telling the truth and he only said again in a businesslike manner:

"You must allow me to manage this in the way which I prefer."

He sat down at the desk and wrote out an 'I.O.U.', and when he had finished he said:

"Now come and sign this and I will give you my address in London. You must promise me, and this is a promise you will keep, to inform me of your whereabouts and what you are doing."

"Yes .. yes .. of course," Miranda agreed. "I .. will do exactly as you tell me to do."

The Earl showed her where to sign and he saw she hesitated before she added her surname to the document.

Then he said as he blotted it:

"You are somewhat remiss in not reading what I have written!"

"I am sorry," Miranda replied abashed. "Shall I do so now?"

He held out the paper to her and she said:

"I understand this amount of francs is the equivalent of not a hundred pounds, but a little over £150."

"You must never sign anything without first reading it," the Earl said. "The extra money is for food, and I want you to promise me that you will feed not only your mother, but also yourself, for if you do not do so, I may never get my money back!"

Miranda made a strange little sound that was half a laugh but which was also very near to tears.

Then she said:

"How can you be so kind .. so wonderful? And how can I ever .. thank you?"

The Earl was silent for a moment. Then he said:

"You can thank me, by giving me your promise."

"To repay you?"

"No, something more than that."

"What is it?"

"I want you to promise me," he answered slowly, "that never again will you think of doing what you suggested to me just now."

He saw the colour come into her cheeks again and he said:

"I understand how you reasoned out for yourself that it was the only way you could manage, but because you are a Lady by birth, because you know it is wrong and in your eyes a sin, it is something you must not contemplate again! Is that understood?"

"I understand .. and I promise," Miranda said. "It was just that I prayed and prayed for days that I could find some way to help Mama, and .. nothing else seemed .. possible."

He did not answer, but merely asked:

"Have you a bank?'

"We did have one when we first came to Paris because Mama thought it safer, but I am afraid there is nothing in our account now."

"Nevertheless, they will honour my cheque. It would be a mistake to walk about with so much money on you in the form of cash. What I will do, Miranda, is to write out this cheque for actually the amount I promised you and give you just enough francs to buy food immediately for your mother and yourself. Then you can withdraw the rest from the bank as you need it."

Because there were tears in Miranda's eyes and her lips were trembling she did not answer.

But he knew that her whole being and everything that vibrated from her expressed her gratitude.

The Earl wrote a cheque, then drew some franc notes from his pocket and laid them on the table.

"Now put them somewhere safe," he said, "and stop at the nearest market so that both you and your mother can have a good meal this evening."

"I will do that."

The Earl considered for a moment whether he should give her the rest of the *pâté* sandwiches, but felt she would consider that an act of charity and resent it.

Instead he said:

"Now our business is transacted, I think we should drink a toast to the future, and as it is a mistake to drink on an empty stomach, I suggest we both have something to eat. It is quite a long time since luncheon."

She did not argue with him, but took another sandwich and he did the same.

When she was not looking he dropped his down the side of his chair from where he knew he could retrieve it later.

He noted, however, and he admired her for it, that while she had eaten, she had taken only the smallest sip of champagne as she said:

"I want to drink a toast to the .. kindest man I have ever .. met."

"Thank you," the Earl said, "and I will drink to a very courageous young woman."

Miranda put down her glass and he said:

"I shall be here in Paris for a little while. Kindly let me know how your mother progresses after the operation has taken place."

"Yes, of course, My Lord, and as soon as she is better I will find work of some sort."

She gave him a shy little smile and added:

"The sort of work of which you would .. approve."

"Good!"

She rose and walked towards the door, turned and added:

"Thank you once .. again from the very .. bottom of my .. heart."

There were tears in her eyes as she spoke and the Earl said quickly:

"You have forgotten one thing."

"What is that?"

"To give me your address."

She hesitated and he knew it was not because she was being secretive, but because she felt ashamed of where they were staying.

"It is," he added quickly, "so that I can let you know if I hear of any position which might suit you."

"Yes, of course," Miranda said quickly, as she wrote down her address on a piece of paper.

"If you want me," she said as she handed it to him, "just send a servant, I will come to you at once."

The Earl was aware that she was afraid of his seeing the squalor in which they had been obliged to live.

To set her mind at rest he said:

"Naturally, that is what I would do," and saw the expression of relief in her eyes.

Then she curtsied and, as if it was impossible to say any more, she went from the room without waiting for him to ring.

Only when she had gone did the Earl think it was the most extraordinary interview he had ever had with a woman in the whole of his life.

As she was so pretty, in fact "lovely" was the right word, it was amazing that living in Paris she had not encountered before now a man who had tried to take advantage of anyone so young and so innocent.

Then he told himself there was no use worrying about the girl.

He had done what he could for her, and he could only congratulate himself on being rather clever in making her accept the money without it hurting her pride.

"Poor little thing!" he said as he walked to the mantelpiece, and wondered what would be the end of the story.

Then as the door opened and his friend the *Vicomte* came in, he decided and the decision rather surprised him, that he had no wish to talk about Miranda or recount what had happened.

CHAPTER TWO

The Earl looked round the Dining-Room with a faint smile of amusement.

No one looking at the table lit with golden candelabra, each with fifteen candles, decorated with large baskets of orchids and crystal glasses glittering like the diamonds round his hostess's neck, could be expected to know that they were being entertained by one of the most famous and the most expensive *horizontales*.

He had met Blanche d'Antigny five years ago, and they had had a few brief fiery nights together before he was obliged to return to London.

It would be ridiculous to say that he had forgotten Blanche, for no one could forget the woman who was one of the celebrities of Paris and who had for four years captivated Russia by her charm and her expertise.

She was, however, thrown out of St. Petersburg when the constant applause and adulation she received had gone to her head and, attired in defiance of protocol, she had attended the traditional Gala performance which ended the winter season at the Opera.

She had been determined to wear a gown in which she would outshine both performers and audience and by sheer bribery had insisted on having one which had been ordered by the Empress.

The next day the Governor of St. Petersburg was commanded to expel her from Russia.

Back in France, she was found by her admirers more seductive and alluring than ever, and the Earl learnt that she had rented a charming *hôtel*, number 11, Avenue de Friedland.

She was, of course, not paying for it herself even though she was earning huge sums on the stage of the *Folies Dramatiques*.

Her official lover was Raphael Bischoffsheim, an enormously rich banker who, the Earl learned when he called at the Avenue de Friedland, had most conveniently gone to a conference of bankers at Lyons.

Blanche welcomed him with open arms.

"I have so often thought of you, *mon brave*," she said with a sincerity it was hard to question, "and now you are here we must lose no time in picking up the threads from where we left off."

The Earl was only too willing to do so.

He not only found Blanche exceedingly seductive as a mistress, but he enjoyed the manner in which, despite her huge success, she was in many ways unspoilt.

At moments she reverted without any embarrassment to the simple peasant-girl, daughter of a carpenter, who until she came to Paris had been perfectly happy in a little town near Bourges in the Indre.

But a wild gambler and *horizontale* in a manner which made her the envy and admiration of the whole of the *demi-monde*, she still said her prayers with intense devotion and, when she had time, attended Mass.

At the moment the Earl was admiring the grace in which she presided over a party which might have been the envy of any Society hostess.

The male guests were all aristocrats of great distinction and they certainly appreciated the *apéritifs* which had been served with blinis and caviar, the superb wines which accompanied the *terrine de foie gras*, the Chablis and Château-Yquem to drink with the lobster and the Château Lafitte with the *poulardes à la gelée*.

Champagne sparkled with the *fraises au kirsch* in silver-gilt goblets, each one in the shape of an animal's head.

Unlike most of the parties which took place in the houses of others, Courtesans like Cora Pearl, the conversation was intelligent and to the Earl's delight and satisfaction was concerned primarily with current affairs.

"Do you really think there will be a war?" he asked one of the guests who not only bore a famous name, but as he was well aware, was *persona grata* with the Emperor and Empress.

"I am afraid it is inevitable," was the reply.

The Earl raised his eye-brows and his informant continued:

"The Emperor is being pushed into being aggressive by his heavy-handed Foreign Secretary, the *Duc* de Gramont."

The Earl smiled.

"The *Duc's* aggressiveness towards the Prussians is, I am told, a personal issue because he has never forgiven Bismarck for calling him 'the stupidest man in Europe'."

"That is true," was the answer, "but it is, above all, the Empress who is determined that we shall fight Germany."

The Earl looked surprised and hoping to elicit more information he said:

"It is unusual for a woman, whether she is an Empress or a peasant, to wish for war."

"Jean is right," another man joined in, "it is the Empress who is anxious for us to fight Prussia."

"I heard that the Emperor is not well," the Earl remarked.

"He is not," somebody answered positively. "He is suffering the tortures of the damned from a stone in the bladder."

The Earl felt in that case it was unlikely he would be willing to go to war.

At the same time, ever since his arrival in Paris, he had found that *'Le Figaro'* published every day editorial articles that were extremely inflammatory.

He had by the end of dinner acquired quite a lot of information which he knew would be of particular interest to Lord Granville and that he must despatch it the next day in a coded letter.

In the meantime it was quite obvious that he would have no time tonight to do anything but reciprocate the ardour which Blanche, without concealment, felt for him.

With a tact that he had not expected of her, she managed to ensure that her guests did not stay too late.

It was not actually a very difficult thing to do, for all of them were paired off with the extremely attractive *demi-mondaines* who had been their partners.

Their seductiveness enhanced by the excellent food and drink made it impossible for any man to resist them.

Almost before he expected it, the Earl found himself in Blanche's bedroom, which he thought might have been described as a Temple for Venus.

Hung with turquoise satin, the four-poster bed with its enormous baldaquin of blue silk and lace-trimmed curtains looked like a throne encircled with mystical clouds.

There was a white bear-skin very soft beneath his feet and, although he was not thinking of it at the moment, he had been told by the gossip columnists in the newspapers that the bath in Blanche's bathroom was made of the finest Carrara marble.

It was reported in *'Le Figaro'* that she had two hundred bottles of mineral water poured into it every time she required a bath because she found that so reviving.

While she enjoyed all this luxury and while her Boulle writing-desk was packed almost to overflowing with jewels, the Earl found it touching that she was never without her little gold crucifix, and on a console table stood an ivory statue of a flagellated Christ.

As she held out her white arms to him, her eyes bright with anticipation and pleasure, he was prepared to swear that, unlike most of her fellow Courtesans, she did not really know the value of money.

She merely enjoyed life and wanted to please those who admired her.

And yet when the Earl walked home as the dawn was breaking and the streets were just beginning to come alive, he found himself thinking not of Blanche, but, strangely enough, of Miranda.

Never, when he was making love to one woman, did he ever allow the thought of another to interfere with his own pleasure and that of the woman to whom he was giving his favours.

Now, however, extraordinary though it seemed, the poverty-stricken girl with her protruding bones and worried eyes kept intruding on his consciousness.

This was so unusual, in fact almost ridiculous, that he supposed the truth must be that Blanche did not attract him as greatly as she had in the past.

But nothing could have been more fiery, more physically satisfying, than the ardour Blanche evoked in him and which certainly had not been diminished by the passage of time since they had last met.

Nevertheless he found himself seeing that worried expression in Miranda's large eyes, hearing the fear in her voice that she would not be able to save her mother.

"I have done my best for the girl," the Earl said as he moved through the deserted streets towards the Champs Elysées.

But he found himself wondering if the operation had been successful, and if the food he had told her to buy had made a difference to her mother and to herself.

He wondered too what Miranda would look like if she were not so thin and emaciated.

When he reached his very comfortable bedroom in the *Vicomte's* house, he found that instead of quickly falling asleep, as he usually did after a night of pleasure, he lay awake for some time watching the first rays of the sun appear on each side of the curtains that covered the windows.

They heralded a new day which would perhaps bring Miranda everything she had desired when she came to him for his help.

"I *have* helped her," he said positively.

And yet still something told him that was not the end of the chapter and that he would sooner or later have to know more.

The next morning, having sent off a long letter which took him some time to write to Lord Granville, he called on the Prince Napoleon who had asked him to do so the first evening he had arrived in Paris.

The Prince Napoleon, known as Plom-Plom, was one of the most controversial, gifted and significant figures in France.

He was, the Earl knew, exceedingly clever, but his political beliefs had remained a problem to his cousin the Emperor ever since the Second Empire had come into being.

The Prince Napoleon had become an Imperial Highness or a Senator in the centre of public affairs.

His private life was as controversial as his public behaviour, and his mistresses were legendary in the way they flaunted themselves in Paris.

The Prince was loved by many women, for despite the fact that he was an ugly man, he was a great charmer and his companionship was sought after by many exceedingly clever men, and the greatest brains in the country met at his house.

To the Earl's delight he found as it was quite early in the morning that the Prince Napoleon was alone and delighted to see him.

Immediately they plunged into a long discussion about the political situation over which the Prince was devastatingly frank and imparted to the Earl information he had not dreamt of receiving.

"War, my dear boy, is inevitable," the Prince said.

"Do you really mean that?" the Earl asked.

"Of course I mean it," Prince Napoleon replied, "and you can blame that damned woman who has about as much sense as a rabbit and, as far as France is concerned, should have been exterminated at birth!"

"Do you mean the Empress?" the Earl asked, being well aware that the Prince had always loathed the Empress Eugenie.

"Of course I mean the Empress!" the Prince snapped. "Only a fool would believe we could win against a country who has the finest and most up-to-date war equipment in the whole of Europe!"

That was what the Earl had thought himself, but it was almost a shock to hear it put so dramatically and so positively by a Frenchman.

"I thought," he said tentatively, "that you had an excellent weapon in the cartridge-firing *chassepot* rifle which has nearly twice the range of the Dreyse 'needle-gun' and I have also heard whispers of a secret weapon called the *mitrailleuse*."

He had, in fact, heard quite a lot about the gun consisting of a bundle of twenty-five barrels which by turning a handle could be fired off in very rapid succession.

The Prince Napoleon laughed.

"Obviously no one has told you," he said, "of the

steel breech-loading cannon which *Herr* Krupp has made for Prussia, but which our thick-headed military leaders have refused to take seriously."

"Well, all I can say," the Earl said as he took his leave, "is that I can only pray that Your Royal Highness is wrong and that we shall, if only by a miracle, continue to enjoy the peace, the beauty, and the charms of Paris together."

Just for a moment there was a frustrated expression in the Prince Napoleon's eyes of a man who knows the truth but cannot make anybody else believe it.

Then he said:

"Time will prove me right, unfortunately, and there is nothing more dangerous than the blindness of those who will not see what is staring them in the face."

As the Earl drove away from the Prince's magnificent house he found himself praying that his predictions were wrong.

If France entered into a war which he had the uncomfortable feeling would be a difficult one to win, they would be deliberately throwing aside all the luxury, the beauty, the extravagance which had made the Second Empire so attractive to *blasé* men like himself, and had produced a very civilised and glamorous Capital.

For eighteen years France had enjoyed a glittering Imperial Régime which, the Earl thought, if politically unstable, had made a brilliant and distinctive contribution to French history.

It was impossible, completely unthinkable, that it should end disastrously, and yet he felt sure that the French had no idea of the determination or the strength of the Germans, and to be defeated by them would be utterly ruinous to the nation.

What was more, he ruminated, war would bring hardship to the working classes of Paris who were suffering already.

Most of the visitors to Paris who merely enjoyed themselves with the *grandes horizontales* were mainly interested in trivial gossip such as that Louis-Napoleon had given the Comtesse de Castiglione a pearl necklace costing four hundred and thirty-two thousand francs, plus fifty thousand francs a month pin-money, or that La Paiva, another *horizontale* spent half a million francs a year on her table.

But the Earl had taken the trouble to study the wages earned by the ordinary French man and woman.

He had learned to his horror that half the population of Paris were living in poverty bordering on destitution, and of these, seventeen thousand women earned no more than fifty centimes to one and a quarter francs a day, for which they were required to labour eleven long hours out of the twenty-four.

The thought sprang to his mind now that, while Miranda had said that as soon as her mother's operation was over she would find some work, it would be a very difficult thing for her to do.

And it was not likely that on one and a quarter francs a day she would be able to repay him what he had loaned her, although he was quite certain that was what she would attempt to do.

Once again he tried to dismiss her from his mind, but he found it impossible throughout the day, while spending his time with the *Vicomte* or visiting other old friends who welcomed him with delight.

When he went in the evening to the *Théâtre des Variétés*, which staged a better show than anything he had seen for a long time, he was still haunted by the anxiety in Miranda's eyes.

Once again he ended the day with Blanche, but this time they dined alone in a private room at the *Café Anglais*.

While the food was delicious and the wine perfect, the Earl found it difficult to forget that the newspapers that day were all full of a garbled account, first published in the German Press, of an interview at Ems between King Wilhelm and the French Ambassador at which the latter made an impertinent demand on the King, who had sharply rebuked him.

"I do not believe they could be such fools!" the Earl exclaimed to the *Vicomte* who brought him further news from one of the Generals concerned with the mobilisation of the Army.

"Nor can I," the *Vicomte* agreed, "but the wretched Emperor is being badgered by the Empress who is determined to teach the Germans a lesson without, like most women, considering the consequences."

Blanche attempted to turn his mind away from anything so serious.

"Let us talk about you, *mon cher*," she said flatteringly. "Now we are together again I realise how much I have missed you, and how no one, not even my charming Russian Prince, has been so perfect and so exciting a lover as you!"

"You flatter me!" the Earl said, being quite prepared however to accept that what she said was the truth.

"I can see you are somewhat *distrait*," Blanche went on, "so let us go home and I will make you think of nothing but *l'amour*, instead of war."

She rose from the table and as he wrapped her satin cloak around her he was conscious of the exotic scent which remained on his skin after he had touched her.

Yet, earlier than usual, the Earl returned to the *Vicomte's* house, and once again before he went to sleep he found himself thinking of Miranda.

"I should imagine the operation is over by now," he thought.

He did not seem to have been asleep for long before his valet called him.

Hicks, who had been with him for some years, came into the room and he knew before the man spoke that he had news which he did not want to hear.

As the curtains were drawn back the Earl sat up in bed and asked:

"What is it, Hicks?"

"France has declared war, M'Lord! The newsvendors are crying it out. I had great difficulty in getting hold of a newspaper for Your Lordship."

"How can the Emperor do anything so crazy!" the Earl said to himself.

Hicks was busy telling him of the wild excitement and exultation that was manifest in the streets.

"They're all intoxicated, M'Lord, with the idea of victory, and there have been mobs everywhere singing the *'Marseillaise'* and shouting *'A Berlin'* and *'Vive la guerre!'*"

When the Earl was up and dressed he found that Hicks had not exaggerated. The mobs were hysterical with excitement, and *'Le Figaro'* opened a subscription fund to present every soldier in the Army with a glass of brandy and a cigar.

At luncheon time the *Vicomte* reported that alleged Prussian spies were being seized and very roughly treated.

"As you are aware, Thornton," he said to the Earl, "the French have loathed the Prussians for years, and the idea of defeating them once and for all is a very heady tonic."

He then said:

"I know you will forgive me if I leave you, but my wife and family will be extremely anxious at the idea of war, especially as two of my wife's brothers are in the French Army. I therefore feel I must go home to the country for a short while."

"But, of course, my dear fellow, I understand!" the Earl said. "Do you want me to leave?"

"Definitely not," the *Vicomte* replied. "Stay for as long as you like. I am sure with so much excitement in the air you will find Paris even gayer than it was before."

The Earl, however, was not thinking of his own pleasure so much as finding out the truth of the situation and sending it to Lord Granville.

He had received this morning a letter from the Foreign Secretary thanking him most profusely for the information which he had already supplied.

The Foreign Secretary begged him to do everything in his power to find out the exact truth of what was occurring and write to him, if possible, every day.

He wrote:

"I cannot stress too forcibly how important at this particular moment your comments are to me. I am relying on you, since my other informants in Paris are, I regret to say, too bemused to be in the slightest degree critical about what they hear from the French Ministers.

"Please, I do beg of you, stay for as long as you

can and keep me informed day by day, or hour by hour, if necessary."

The Earl thought that in the circumstances it would be very difficult for him to refuse to do what Lord Granville wanted.

He had, in the past, been so useful to the Foreign Secretary that he knew his reputation there stood very high.

He was aware that if he returned to England immediately he would disappoint the whole Cabinet, including the Prime Minister.

"I shall certainly stay for as long as I can," he said aloud to the *Vicomte*.

"I am sure you will never be in any danger in Paris," the *Vicomte* laughed, "and everything I possess, including my cellar, is at your disposal."

"Thank you," the Earl said. "I can only promise to reciprocate your hospitality when you come to England."

The *Vicomte* had gone leaving the Earl alone, and he knew that for his own peace of mind he had to see Miranda.

He found it impossible to go on simultaneously thinking about her and trying to erase her from his thoughts.

It would, he decided, be far easier once and for all to call to see her instead of speculating about what had happened.

He therefore drove in the *Vicomte's* smart carriage to the address she had given him.

He had guessed that it would be in a part of Paris not yet destroyed by Baron Haussmann's design for a new City.

There were still large areas of Paris that were waiting to be demolished, and this was where those who required really cheap lodgings could find accommodation.

The Earl was, therefore, not surprised when he found the carriage entering streets that were narrow and extremely dirty.

In fact, as he had suspected, the high rents charged in Haussmann's new City had gradually forced the workers into what had become slums as evil as those that had been demolished.

The house at which the horses drew up was literally crumbling into dust, and the Earl realised it was a lodging-house.

With some difficulty a slatternly woman, who was the *concierge*, was extracted from the basement to inform him that *Mademoiselle* Valmont was on the top floor.

"I hope, *Monsieur*, when you get there," she said impertinently, "you aren't too tired to enjoy what you came for!"

She laughed at her own joke and with a lewd gesture disappeared once more into the darkness of the basement.

Because the Earl was athletic he did not find the stairs to the sixth floor particularly tiring.

He realised, however, that it would be impossible for anybody who was as ill as Miranda had said her mother was, to climb up and down such mountainous heights without collapsing.

He reached the top landing and knocked on the door nearest to the staircase.

For a moment there was no answer. Then a soft voice he recognised said, "*Entrez!*" in a tone which told him that Miranda was surprised that she should have a visitor.

He opened the door and saw her sitting on the side of an iron bedstead which, with another one beside it, had been pulled into the centre of the room.

The Earl was aware this was because of the rats that were to be found in every building as dilapidated as this.

They became so bold that they would climb onto a table or worry the feet of the sleeping occupants in bed.

Inside the room the peeling wallpaper revealed the crumbling plaster on the walls, the window had several cracked panes of glass, there was scarcely any furniture, and no covering of any sort on the wooden floor.

The sight of such squalor was so horrifying to him that Miranda's white skin and even her emaciated wrists seemed almost beautiful in contrast.

Then as he realised she was staring at him with tears in her eyes and an expression on her face he found no difficulty in interpreting, he knew what had happened without her having to tell him.

"Your mother?" he asked and was aware of the answer before she replied:

"M.Mama .. died this morning .. before they could operate on .. her."

Her voice broke as she spoke and she put up her hands to her eyes in a desperate effort, the Earl knew, to control the tears that were threatening to overcome her.

Then as she forced herself not to make a scene she asked in a voice that trembled:

"Why .. are you .. h.here? I .. I thought you would send .. a s.servant if you .. wanted me."

"I preferred to come myself," the Earl replied, "and I think, Miranda, that it is a good thing that I did so. What are you going to do now?"

"First I have to see to Mama's .. Funeral .. which will take place .. tomorrow," Miranda answered. "After that .. I must find myself some .. work."

"I thought that was what you were thinking of doing," the Earl said. "But, as I expect you know, war has been declared, and I think it will be even more difficult than it is already for you to find yourself any sort of reasonable employment."

Miranda gave a little gasp, then she said:

"I .. I have most of your .. money left."

"I do not suppose that will last long!" the Earl said.

He saw the consternation in her voice and feeling he was making things worse for her than they were already, he looked away from her and saw to his surprise that hanging on the filthy walls were two pictures.

They were a very striking contrast to the dirt that made everything else seem grey and sordid.

As if to give Miranda time to think he moved towards the pictures saying as he did so:

"I suppose these were painted by your father."

"No .. one would .. buy them," Miranda said with a little sob in her voice.

The Earl stood looking at them and could understand that they would not be to the taste of the average person who wanted something pretty to ornament their rooms.

One picture was of leafless trees in winter beside a dark pool of water in which they were dimly reflected, and there was something harsh about the way in which the picture had been painted.

The other was of a farm yard with chickens pecking for food amongst a pile of litter and an ancient dog asleep in the sunshine.

Both the pictures were realistic but far from attractive.

At the same time, the Earl thought, the artist undoubtedly had some talent, if not a great deal of it.

Then, as he saw the signature scrawled rather dashingly in the bottom right-hand corner of each picture, he stiffened.

He stared at it, then he said:

"Kyle? Lionel Kyle? Was that your father's name?"

"Y..yes."

Miranda stammered the answer and after a moment the Earl asked:

"Then you must be a relative of mine! Why did you not tell me?"

"I .. I did not .. think you would want to .. help after the .. family refused to have anything to do with Papa .. because he had .. run away with my mother."

The Earl was silent, remembering that the behaviour of Lionel Kyle, his father's first cousin, had caused a great scandal in the family.

He had run away the night before his wedding because he had fallen in love with a French girl.

The Earl had been too young at the time to understand what had happened, but he remembered the family talking about it for years afterwards and saying what a disgrace it had been.

The jilted bride had been the daughter of the Marquess of Dorset, Lord Lieutenant of the County and a man of considerable power and influence at Court.

It had caused a great rift between the Marquess and

the Kyle family, and the Earl could remember his father denouncing his cousin for having behaved like a cad, and swearing that he would never allow him to set foot inside the family mansion again.

That, however, was something Lionel had never attempted to do, for he had left for France and the girl he loved.

But the Earl had never imagined in his wildest dreams that he would ever encounter either Lionel Kyle or any of his family.

Now he turned round to see that Miranda was looking at him fearfully, and she said in a very young and trembling little voice:

"I .. I am sorry .. very .. sorry."

"You can hardly be held responsible for the actions of your father!" the Earl replied. "But whatever you may say, you should have told me, when you came to see me, who you were."

"I .. I thought about it .. but I was afraid you would refuse .. to help me."

"Yet you approached me because I was a relative."

"Papa, however harshly they treated him, always talked of his family with pride and affection," Miranda said. "He had a great admiration for your father and knew how distressed his behaviour would make him. But he knew that if he could not marry Mama .. he would be unhappy for the .. rest of his life."

The quite simple way Miranda spoke was rather touching and the Earl said:

"This puts a very different complexion on our relationship, Miranda. You must realise that."

"Y.you mean .. you will not .. help me after all .. and you .. want your m.money back?"

The fear in her eyes told the Earl more effectively

than her words what she was feeling and he said quickly:

"No, of course not. But as a member of my family you are now my responsibility, and I not only cannot leave you here in this ghastly house, which I would not have done anyway, but as war has been declared, I cannot leave you in Paris!"

Miranda looked at him as if she did not understand.

Then she asked in a hesitating voice:

"Then .. what am I .. to do?"

"I am going to take you back to England with me," the Earl replied. "We will talk about it in more salubrious surroundings than we are doing at the moment."

"I .. I did not .. wish you to .. see this place," Miranda said. "I knew it would .. shock you .. but it was all we could .. afford."

The Earl's lips tightened.

It seemed to him inconceivable that any member of his family should have been reduced to living in the sort of place he would not have thought fit for one of his animals.

"Come along," he said, "and bring with you your father's pictures, if you wish to keep them."

Miranda looked round her a little wildly.

"I .. I must pack my .. other things, and .. Mama's."

"I cannot believe there is anything worth keeping," the Earl answered. "Leave them behind. As your Guardian, for that is what I now am, the first thing I have to do is to buy you some decent clothes."

He saw her eyes widen and added:

"While I respected your pride, Miranda, now it is correct for me to look after you, and correct for you to accept what I will give you."

Miranda did not answer.

She looked at him for a long moment as if she could hardly believe what he was saying.

Then as he opened the door she sped across the room to take down the two pictures painted by her father and carry them under her arm to join the Earl at the top of the staircase.

He thought with a secret smile that few women would have taken him quite so literally or so sensibly, but Miranda walked beside him as obediently as one of his dogs might have done.

Only when he had helped her into the carriage did he realise as the sun glinted on her hair that she had come away without a bonnet, obeying him to the letter that she should bring with her only the pictures.

The horses and the carriage which had evoked a lot of attention from the other inhabitants of the street, set off quickly, as if they were glad to be away from such an unpleasant neighbourhood.

Then, as they drew into a large Square, there was a huge crowd of men, women and children, celebrating the announcement of war with cries of, "*Vive la guerre!*"

As the sound came wafting towards them Miranda asked:

"Will the French win?"

"I am hoping so," the Earl admitted. "At the same time the German Army is larger and very much better trained."

"If we lose," Miranda said as if she spoke to herself, "Mama would be .. very upset."

The Earl wanted to reply that in that case she would not know about it, but he thought that would seem heartless and he merely said:

"The English are on the whole more pro-German than pro-French."

"How can they be?" Miranda asked indignantly.

The Earl wondered if he should go into the obvious explanation that the English Royal Family were mostly of German origin and Queen Victoria had always considered the French an immoral race. Her opinion had not altered on meeting Louis-Napoleon before he became Emperor.

He decided, however, that this was not the moment for a history lesson and he merely said:

"I think, as the British will be neutral in the war, that is what you and I must try to be."

Miranda glanced up at him as if she knew that he was deliberately evading the question.

Then they drove out of the Square into other streets where flags were being flown out of the windows and once again there was an atmosphere of wild rejoicing.

The Earl found himself wondering what the people's reaction would be if, as he expected, the news from the battlefield was not as good as they hoped.

He kept remembering that he had heard and had already reported to London that the Germans had four hundred thousand men concentrated on the far side of the Rhine.

His informant had added, as if deliberately to accentuate the contrast:

"The French are only able to muster two hundred and fifty thousand."

The Earl was, however, concerned for the moment with Miranda, and when they arrived at the house in the Champs Elysées, he informed the Steward that he wished to speak to the Housekeeper.

While waiting for her he and Miranda moved into

the same Sitting-Room in which they had talked the first time she had called on him.

She looked around and said:

"This is a very fine and beautiful house! I described it to Mama and she said it reminded her of the Château my grandmother lived in as a girl."

"It is time you told me more about yourself," the Earl said. "Where did you live in France when your father was alive?"

"In the country," Miranda replied, "a little way south of Paris in a small village, and although we were poor, we were very, very happy."

She gave him a shy smile as she said:

"I am sure your relatives would never believe it, but Papa never regretted running away with Mama. They loved each other so much ... and he often said he would have been miserable with the grand bride his father had chosen for him and who was very prim and proper."

"And who was your mother?" the Earl asked.

"Her father was the youngest son of the *Comte* de Valmont who unfortunately had very little money. So Mama, which I dare say you would have thought outrageous, taught in a School so that she could help her family."

"How did she meet your father?"

"It was very romantic! Mama had taken some of the School-children for a treat to see the Zoo in Paris, and she was looking at the antics of the monkeys when one of them threw an over-ripe plum through the bars of the cage which hit one of the spectators on the nose! It was so funny that despite herself Mama laughed, and she found a gentleman beside her was laughing too."

"Who I suppose was your father," the Earl finished.

"It was. He always said they were introduced by laughing together, and they continued to laugh together all through their .. lives."

Miranda gave a little sigh that was very wistful as she said:

"That is what I have missed these past years – laughing with Papa and hearing Mama laugh as well."

The Earl was unable to reply for at that moment the door opened and the Housekeeper came in.

She was a severe-looking woman, but very efficient, and as soon as the Earl explained that he had found one of his cousins who had just been orphaned by her mother's death, she was sympathetic and took Miranda upstairs.

The Earl then sat down at a desk and wrote letters to several Couturiers with whom he was acquainted in Paris, having on previous visits bought a number of gowns for the mistress with whom he was involved at the time.

He told them to bring a whole selection of clothes to the house first thing in the morning for a very thin, young girl.

He sent the notes by a footman, then waited for Miranda to return to him.

When she did so she was to his surprise, dressed in a very attractive afternoon gown with a bustle which she explained hastily belonged to the *Vicomte's* sister, who had left it behind the last time she was staying in Paris, and had been lent to her by the Housekeeper.

"I hope she will not .. mind my borrowing her gown," Miranda said in a worried voice, "but the Housekeeper assures me that she has in fact, dispensed with this garment altogether, and said it could be thrown away as she had no further use for it."

"It will certainly keep you covered until some clothes of your own arrive," the Earl replied, "which I have already ordered for you."

"You have?" Miranda asked quickly in surprise.

Unexpectedly she went down on her knees beside the chair in which the Earl was sitting.

"Please," she said, "I do not want to be an encumbrance or a trouble. I realise how very kind you are being in bringing me here, but to avoid any embarrassment when you go back to England, I could return to the village where we lived before Mama and I came to Paris."

The Earl did not speak and after a moment with the colour coming into her face she said:

"I .. I am afraid I would .. have to ask you to give me a little .. money until I can .. earn some .. but I would promise to .. return it as soon as .. possible."

The Earl looked at her and said:

"I think, Miranda, you realise that our arrangement is very different now that I am your Guardian. I intend to look after you and I shall take you back with me to England, where you will live with one of our many relatives whom I know would be only too pleased to have you."

He gave a short laugh as he added:

"We have a wide choice because there are a great number of Kyles – I often think too many of them! – and I promise I will find you someone really charming who will look after you and see that sooner or later you marry a husband who will have no wish to run away from you the night before the wedding!"

Miranda gave a little cry before she expostulated:

"That is unkind! Perhaps none of your relatives will have me because they will still be shocked at the way Papa behaved."

"I can assure you," the Earl replied, "that the great majority of them have forgotten it ever happened, but those who do remember will doubtless think it very romantic, especially when they see you."

"I hope you are right," Miranda said, "but things like that are not .. always easily .. forgotten."

The Earl knew this was true and thought it rather sensible of her to think in that way.

Then as if the fact that she was kneeling at his feet made him feel embarrassed he said:

"Leave everything to me. I will enjoy organising your life for you, and I promise you that in the future it will be a very happy one."

CHAPTER THREE

Because he was aware that Miranda was very tired, the Earl sent her to bed before dinner, which suited him as he had already arranged to dine with the Prince Napoleon at the house of one of his friends.

It was an all-male dinner, and he enjoyed it because the conversation was stimulating and witty and, of course, what concerned him more, it was about the war.

The French were, as he expected, elated at the thought of defeating the Prussians.

At the same time, the Prince Napoleon, if no one else, was pessimistic about the outcome of the whole conflict.

He said sourly:

"The Emperor is riding at the head of his Army with that woman's last words: 'Louis, do your duty well!' still ringing in his ears! But there is not a single Army Corps up to full strength."

For a moment there was silence, then everybody began to try to find statistics to prove that the Prince Imperial was wrong.

As they sat very late talking and arguing, the Earl did not go to visit Blanche as he had intended, but returned to the *Vicomte's* house.

He had found himself thinking of Miranda several times during the evening.

He thought how brave she had been over her mother's death and knew there were few women of his acquaintance who would have behaved with such dignity and self-control.

He had already told his secretary to make arrangements for the Funeral to take place late the next morning, which would now, of course, be very different from what the doctor had intended when Miranda left it in his hands.

Then, her mother would only have had what was little more than a pauper's funeral, but now the Earl had given orders that everything was to be done to make the Service as pleasant as possible for Miranda and had told his secretary to order flowers, and that the priest who officiated was to be paid.

He had postponed the time of the Service so that he would be able to buy Miranda a decent gown to wear, and as he expected, she, out of habit, came down to breakfast early having always lived in the country.

When they were alone, he said to her:

"I have a suggestion to put to you, Miranda, which I hope will not upset you."

She looked at him apprehensively and he said:

"The Couturiers will be arriving at any moment, and I intend to buy you one black gown to wear today at your mother's Funeral. But because I know black will not suit you while you are so thin and pale, I am suggesting, if it will not upset you, that you should not continue to wear mourning."

To his surprise Miranda replied:

"I am so glad you feel like that. When Papa died we could not afford to buy black, and Mama said she was glad, feeling it was hypocritical to make a great show of grief when we were actually only crying for ourselves."

She paused to see if the Earl understood and explained:

"Mama knew Papa was not dead, but only waiting for her somewhere where she could join him, as she has done now."

Because Miranda spoke quite simply with a sincerity which was very moving, she made the Earl hold out his hand to her.

As Miranda put hers into his he said:

"I think you are very brave and very sensible. You shall have the most attractive clothes that Paris can supply you with, although I am afraid we shall not have long to enjoy them here as we have to return to England."

He knew by the expression on Miranda's face, although she did not say anything, that she would much rather stay in Paris with him.

But he was aware that he would have to return to England with Miranda rather sooner than he expected.

However, although he knew how much he was helping Lord Granville with his reports, there was no violent hurry about it.

After breakfast the Couturiers arrived and the Earl gave them precise instructions as to what was required.

One of them hastily went back to the shop to produce a black gown for Miranda to wear at the Funeral, and although it was definitely a gown for mourning, it was very different from what an English dressmaker would have produced.

Miranda found the gown when she was dressed had a *chic*, and also something young, about it which could only have come from a French designer.

The small bonnet to go with it, with velvet ribbons and a light veil was, the Earl thought, very appropriate for the occasion.

They went to the Cemetery, and the Service which took place in the little Chapel was lightened by the mass of flowers his secretary had ordered on his behalf and relieved the gloom and depression which the Earl always associated with Funerals.

It was a tense moment when the coffin was lowered into the ground, and he found Miranda's hand slipped into his as if she felt she must hold onto somebody.

But she did not cry and once again the Earl commended her courage and her control.

Only when they had driven away in a closed carriage did she say in a tremulous little voice:

"I .. I shall .. miss Mama terribly! But I know .. she will be very glad that I am .. with you .. and that you have been .. so kind to me .. it is what .. Papa would have .. wanted .. too."

The Earl found it difficult to answer, knowing that she was fighting her tears, but the tension was lifted as they passed a mob of people screaming, *"Vive la guerre!"* waving flags, and finding the occasion a good opportunity for making a general nuisance of themselves.

The afternoon was spent in trying on the clothes which the models and Couturiers had brought for the Earl to see, and arguing, as he had expected, over the different materials and the manner in which the evening gowns should be decorated.

They produced one gown after another and discussed them, the Earl thought, as a *Maître d'Hôtel* in France would do when one ordered a meal. But he quite understood that it was impossible for Miranda to take any part in what was going on.

Finally when the Couturiers withdrew, all smiles, at the orders they had received, the Earl realised that Miranda was looking very tired and sent her upstairs to lie down.

It was only then that she asked wistfully:

"Shall I see you .. again this .. evening?"

The Earl hesitated and she added quickly:

"Please .. I do not wish to be a nuisance .. in any way .. and I know you have hundreds of .. friends in Paris who must be .. longing to be with you."

The Earl contemplated whether he should dine with Miranda and go to see Blanche afterwards.

Then he thought he might leave her to have dinner in bed and spend his time with Blanche.

He had, however, not heard from the alluring *horizontale* although he had told his secretary to send her a large basket of orchids first thing this morning with apologies for not calling on her last night, as he had intended.

After a moment's hesitation he said to Miranda:

"Let me answer that question a little later. I suggest you go upstairs now and sleep, and I will let you know in an hour or two exactly what we are doing."

She flashed him a smile that erased the worry from her eyes and the lines from round her mouth, and went from the room.

"The more she rests, the better," the Earl assuaged his conscience.

Ordering the carriage, he set off to visit Blanche.

She was, as he expected, at home, and as it was what the French call *"cinq à sept"* she was in her four-poster bed looking exquisitely alluring and very like the magnificent picture that Paul Baudry had painted of her as *"The Repentent Magdalen"*.

She held out her arms as the Earl appeared and cried with a lilt in her voice:

"I thought you had forgotten me!"

"I could never do that!" the Earl said, kissing first one hand, then the other and sitting down on a chair that was conveniently placed beside the bed.

"You must forgive me for being so remiss in not coming to you last night, but I was with the Prince Imperial. You know how his dinners always seem endless, although actually, last night, everything that was said was extremely important."

"I missed you, *mon brave!*" Blanche said.

She was far too experienced with men to reproach him and she only added:

"Bisch," which was what she always called Raphael Bischoffsheim, "tells me he is returning tomorrow, and he thinks it is right of me to move out of Paris."

The Earl stiffened.

"Move out of Paris?" he asked. "Does he think it is dangerous?"

"He does not sound very happy," Blanche replied, "and I know that before he left he and a number of his Banker friends were absolutely convinced that war would be a disaster."

The Earl knew that Raphael Bischoffsheim was an extremely shrewd man, and if his opinion and that of his friends echoed that of the Prince Napoleon, the future of France certainly looked gloomy.

He did not say so to Blanche, but merely consoled her in a very practical manner, enjoying the ensuing two hours in a manner which the French had always advocated.

Later, when it was possible to talk, he said, lying back against the lace-edge pillows:

"If you are thinking of leaving Paris, where will you go?"

"Bisch has bought a very attractive Château for me in the Loire Valley and, although I shall enjoy being with him, I shall not stay there a moment longer than is necessary."

She gave a little laugh as she said:

"You know how much I love the Theatre, and after all, I am an actress."

The Earl was aware that she was not a particularly good one.

But when she had appeared naked in an Operetta by Herve, singing although she had no voice, gaily throwing diamonds about, she lit up the whole theatre with an infectious magic which the audience found irresistible.

"Paris will not be the same without you," the Earl said.

Because she wanted him to praise her, Blanche cuddling close to him read aloud what Charles Dignet had said about her in his sensual anthology "*Les Jolies Femmes de Paris*".

"Blanche d'Antigny has the bosom of Antiope and the head of a Bacchante. The famous head is proudly attached to plump milk-white shoulders moulded like those of Rubens' goddesses. Her cheeks have cast the lilies to the winds and kept only the roses, those flowers of passion. The eyes, almost childlike, have the fixity of sparkling minerals. The sensual mouth was made to sing or drain a glass of champagne, the wine of love."

After she had finished reading it the Earl threw back his head and laughed.

"Perfect!" he said. "It describes you completely and that is how I shall always remember you."

He knew he had pleased her, but as he spoke he found himself thinking about Miranda waiting to hear if she could dine with him or not.

He thought he could see her eyes quite clearly beseeching him like a child, longing for a special treat.

The Earl threw off the scented sheets and got out of bed.

"You are not leaving me?" Blanche cried. "This will be our last night together."

"Alas, I cannot dine with you," the Earl replied, "but because it is our last night, I will come to you after supper."

He started to dress and because Blanche did not reply he said:

"I am sure there is no necessity for you to be alone in my absence."

"That is true," Blanche agreed. "There are two extremely charming gentlemen waiting in case I should be free, but, *mon cher*, I would so much rather be with you."

"And I with you," the Earl replied, "but I have a duty to perform that I cannot set on one side."

"I understand," Blanche said in a soft voice, "but you will not forget to join me later?"

She gave a deep sigh as she said:

"There have been men in my life, but not one can compare with you."

The Earl took his leave of her, and as soon as he returned he sent a servant upstairs to Miranda to say that he would be dining with her in an hour's time.

He thought as he sent the message that he could almost see the light that would come into her eyes and the excitement with which she would get up to dress.

When he went to his own room where Hicks was waiting for him he confessed if slightly wryly, that this was the first time in his life that he had ever set his own desires on one side in order to please somebody else.

Then he told himself that it would be cruel to leave Miranda alone when she knew no one in Paris, and if he did not dine with her, unlike Blanche she would have a dismal meal with no one to share it.

He bathed and dressed and went downstairs, looking very resplendent in his evening-clothes and was not surprised to find Miranda already waiting for him.

She was wearing a gown that he had bought her because it was ready-made, and as it was a model, it fitted her because she was so slender.

He realised as soon as he entered the Salon that she was feeling self-conscious and at the same time anxious that he should appreciate her appearance.

As she looked up at him beseechingly he said:

"You certainly look very different from the first time I saw you!"

"You are .. pleased?"

"I think it is very becoming."

She gave a little sigh.

"I was afraid you might be .. disappointed after you had taken so much .. trouble over me."

"We shall see the results of our labours," the Earl said, "when the gowns we have ordered so painstakingly materialise. Then I must take you out and show you Paris, and see if you find it as enchanting as you expect."

There was an unmistakable radiance in her eyes as she said:

"That would be .. wonderful! But you are quite sure it will not bore you?"

Before he could reply she went on:

"I know how elegant .. besides being witty and amusing .. the ladies are with whom you usually spend your time in Paris .. and I am very conscious that I cannot .. compete with them."

"I would not expect you to do so," the Earl replied.

As he spoke he thought of Blanche and how voluptuously she had behaved only an hour or two ago, and he continued:

"As my relative, Miranda, and as a Kyle, you are very different from those you think of as 'The Ladies of Paris'. They are actually not even spoken of by most Englishwomen, and certainly not by someone as young as yourself."

He saw the colour come into her pale cheeks as if she realised he was rebuking her, and she said:

"I .. I am sorry .. I am afraid I shall .. make a great many .. mistakes .. which may .. annoy you."

She drew in her breath before she went on:

"Perhaps it would be .. better if I did not go to .. England .. but stayed in France."

"That is ridiculous!" the Earl said. "Of course you will come to England with me. I am only telling you that many things which happen commonly in France would be best forgotten, especially when you are with our relatives, many of whom have very strict ideas of propriety."

"You are frightening me!"

"I have no wish to do that," the Earl said, "and I promise I will look after you and help you."

"But you will not always be there," she said reasonably.

"Then I will find somebody to take my place whom you can trust."

He could see by her expression that she thought it impossible that anyone could take his place, but she did not say so aloud.

He told himself that he must be very careful not to become so important to her that she fell in love with him and was unhappy when they were apart.

It was what had happened to so many other women in the past and he had no wish for a child like Miranda to look on him as anything but the head of the family, her Guardian, or rather a father figure, who would help and protect her.

He could not help, however, being aware, while they were eating the excellent dinner which the *Vicomte's* Chef had prepared for them, that she was listening to him with a rapt attention.

And although she had plenty to contribute to any subject they discussed she always deferred to his opinion.

He found that she was very intelligent and

surprisingly well read. So without having intended to, he found himself telling her what he had heard last night at the dinner-party and how pessimistic the Prince Napoleon as well as the Bankers were at the idea of war.

He knew she was horrified at the idea of a Prussian victory, though at the same time she was perceptive enough to realise it was a strong possibility.

"I read in one newspaper," she said, "that King Wilhelm is the first professional soldier to rule Prussia since Frederick the Great. It has been rumoured that he can inspect eighty-seven Battalions in twenty-two days!"

"Where did you learn that?" the Earl asked, thinking it was something which would interest Lord Granville.

"I think it was in *'Le Jour'*," Miranda replied. "But *'Le Figaro'* always laughs at the Prussians and boasts that the French could easily knock them off the face of the earth."

"A dangerous optimism," the Earl said drily.

It was something he was to repeat to himself nearly three weeks later when Paris went mad with excitement on learning that the Emperor had captured Saarbrücken from the weak German advance forces.

All Paris revelled in the triumph, and at the news that the fourteen-year-old Prince Imperial had had his baptism of fire, picking up as a souvenir a Prussian bullet that fell near him.

A telegram was read out on the Bourse falsely reporting the capture of the Prussian Crown Prince by Marshall MacMahon, and enraptured Parisians made a famous tenor sing the *Marseillaise* from the top of a horse-drawn bus.

The elation was tremendous and the Earl as he moved

among his many friends, especially those in the Ministry, hoped that their almost incoherent rejoicing would not be short-lived.

Because he was so busy listening to what everybody had to say, picking up pieces of information to send to London, he was obliged to leave Miranda in the charge of a servant.

The Housekeeper, under his instructions, had procured for her a very pleasant and experienced Lady's-maid who could accompany her to her fittings with the Couturiers, and could also be trusted to help her choose the bonnets, bags, shoes, and gloves and all the other accessories that the Earl had listed as being essential in a fashionable young lady's wardrobe.

She was therefore not left alone, but whenever he returned she welcomed him eagerly and, because she begged him to do so, he told her a great deal of what he had heard.

He had learned with some surprise that she read every newspaper, having asked the Steward to make sure that each one was brought to her as soon as it was issued.

As the Prince Napoleon had expected, the rejoicing was short-lived.

The first blow fell at daybreak on the 4th August when a division in MacMahon's Army was caught breakfasting at Wissembourg in Alsace by troops of the Crown Prince.

The French fought heroically but were overrun by sheer weight of numbers, and became demoralised when their General was killed by a shell.

But this was still only a skirmish. The main blow fell two days later at Woerth when General MacMahon, deceived as to the number the Prussians could bring against them, allowed himself to be brought to battle by the Crown Prince, with more than twice as many infantry as himself.

The result was a resounding French defeat though the Prussians suffered so heavily that they could not follow up the fugitives.

On the same day, the other half of the French forces, optimistically entitled "The Army of the Rhine" and commanded by the Emperor himself, suffered an equally crushing defeat at Spickeren, north of the Vorges.

Now a kind of depression seemed to fall like a fog over Paris, and while Frenchmen kept saying it was only a question of re-grouping the French forces, the Earl learned that a general withdrawal had begun.

Now he began to wonder if Bisch had not been wise in taking Blanche out of Paris, and whether he would be sensible to leave himself with Miranda before things became difficult.

He was not quite certain what this would mean. At the same time, every day those who really were aware of what was taking place became more gloomy.

There was no doubt that the instructions, orders and counter-orders, that went out from Paris were almost being panic-stricken.

The over-optimism of the first few weeks of the war had been replaced by a very much darker mood and, in the Earl's opinion, many of the Parisians were in a state bordering upon madness.

Coming back from a luncheon which had been like a Funeral Wake, he saw three or four German residents being almost kicked to death and only saved by the intervention of the Police.

The mob had now become excited in a different

mood and were often being extremely destructive. Driving through Paris, he noticed that the larger Cafés were being forced to close.

Coming home the next afternoon he found Miranda awaiting his arrival in the hall.

As soon as she saw him she ran towards him and pulled him into the Salon where they could not be overheard.

"What is it?" the Earl asked sharply.

"The servants say the Prussians will be arriving in Paris at any moment, and the Steward learned today that the roads have been blocked by fortifications."

"I am sure things are not as bad as that!" the Earl replied calmly.

He was aware however that the Parisians were extremely jittery, and no one was quite certain what was happening as reports from the battlefield were contradictory or often failed to arrive at all.

He had also been told by some extreme Republicans that there was a serious insurrection in the working-class quarter of La Villette where the houses were very much the same as the one in which he had found Miranda.

A Fire-station had been attacked in an effort to acquire arms and several firemen had been killed.

When he left Miranda, the Earl sent for Hicks.

The man had been with him for so many years that he trusted his judgement in many things and he asked now:

"What do you think we should do, Hicks?"

The valet who had a very shrewd idea of the Earl's value to Lord Granville said:

"Things is getting very nasty, M'Lord, but I don't think they're half as bad as them Froggies is making out."

"Do they really think that Paris might be besieged?"

"They might believe anything!" Hicks said laconically. "But if Your Lordship asks me, I wouldn't be surprised if that wasn't what them Prussians is aiming for."

The Earl thought the same thing and he made up his mind.

"I tell you what we had better do, Hicks," he said. "I think you should go ahead with the luggage as soon as you are ready, which would make it easier when we have to leave for Miss Miranda and I to travel light."

"I sees your point, M'Lord," Hicks said. "I'll get everything packed, but there's no need for us as is English to be in any hurry. I know Your Lordship wants to remain for as long as possible."

The Earl made no comment, thinking it was impossible to keep anything from Hicks who actually handed his letters to the Couriers to take to London.

He wrote another describing as clearly as possible everything that he had recently heard, but, even as he wrote it, he wondered if it was the true picture.

Then a few days later he was told by Prince Napoleon, before it was known elsewhere in Paris, that the Emperor had arrived at Chalons in a third-class railway carriage to find all the signs of a beaten Army.

"I am told," the Prince said, "that exhausted soldiers lay about vegetating rather than living, and the Officer who brought me the information told me they scarcely moved, even if one kicked them!"

"I can hardly believe it!" the Earl said.

"In fact," the Prince went on, "discipline, I am told, hardly exists, and the eighteen Battalions of the Gardes Mobiles from Paris are having to be dug out of brothels and drinking places to be sent back."

The Earl was speechless and the Prince Napoleon continued:

"My cousin, not before time, has called a conference at which the fate of the Empire is to be decided. I am leaving immediately to be with him. God knows, it is now too late for anyone to listen to me when they would not listen before."

The Earl felt that what the Prince Imperial had told him was like a blow, and leaving the Prince's house he drove home in a very sombre mood.

"I am sure," he said to Hicks, without any explanation, "we should be leaving for England."

"They say in the streets, M'Lord, that the Emperor's been defeated," Hicks said.

The Earl did not answer because he could not dare to confirm aloud even to his servant what the Prince Imperial had told him, and he was already aware how much it would distress Miranda.

To take his mind, and hers, off what was happening, he decided to take her to the Theatre and sent a servant to the Opera House to book a box for whatever performance was taking place there.

Miranda was thrilled, as he knew she would be.

What made it even more exciting was that one of the prettiest evening-gowns had arrived which she was longing to show the Earl.

When she came into the Salon where he was waiting he thought she certainly looked very different from the miserable, starved girl who had come to him with such a fantastic proposition.

He remembered how he had loaned her £150, having no idea whether he would ever see her again.

She was still pitifully thin, but the good food and

rest had already softened the sharp line of her chin and the protruding bones at her wrists.

Her eyes still seemed enormous in her small face, but because she was happy they shone like stars, and it struck him that when she was fully recovered she would undoubtedly be a beauty.

He was however so intent on thinking of what he had learnt from the Prince Imperial that he deliberately took Miranda to a small but charming Restaurant in the Palais Royal where the food was superlative but there were no other distractions.

She was entranced, as he knew she would be, with the decor, the elegance of the other diners, and although she could eat very little, finding it still difficult after starving for so long to absorb much food, she was very appreciative of the culinary skill evident in everything they consumed.

When dinner was finished the Earl put over her shoulders the wrap that went with her gown and helped her into the carriage which was waiting outside.

They drove to the Opera House and when they reached it and had just started, with a number of other playgoers to walk up the steps to the brilliantly lighted entrance, they were subjected to the jeers of a mob of noisy toughs.

They were shouting rude, personal remarks and, what was to the Earl more sinister than anything he had heard up until now a chant of "Down with the Empire".

He was well aware there was a great deal of opposition to the Emperor amongst the more revolutionary Republicans, who were suffering most from the difficulties which had already arisen at the outbreak of war and the appalling conditions in which they were housed.

He put his hand under Miranda's elbow to guide her up the steps but as he did so, a scuffle broke out on the steps just ahead of them, when a gentleman struck one of the mob with his cane and the rest moved in threateningly.

Aware of the danger, the Earl looked back to see if it would be wise to return to their carriage before it drove away, but it was impossible to do anything but try to go forward.

The jostling around them grew more violent and as he felt Miranda tremble and move closer to him he knew how frightened she was.

Then fists began to fly as the gentleman with the cane began to lay about him indiscriminately, knocking down one of the yelling youths who was blocking his way.

"I must get you out of here!" the Earl said to Miranda.

As he was wondering how he could do so, a brick thrown with a violence that made it lethal caught him on the side of the head.

It knocked off his hat and he fell as if poleaxed.

As he slipped towards the ground, his body brushing against the people just in front of them, Miranda screamed.

Then, as he lay there unconscious, she screamed again.

CHAPTER FOUR

The Earl stirred and somebody came to his side to ask very softly:

"Are you thirsty?"

The Earl heard the words, but he could not understand them.

Then he felt his head being gently raised and a vessel lifted to his lips and he drank a little, although it was difficult to swallow.

Then as his head went back against the pillows he felt himself drifting away into a darkness, though as he went he had the feeling that Miranda was beside him.

The Earl awoke, opened his eyes, and for a moment wondered where he was and what had happened.

Then an excited voice exclaimed:

"You are awake! Can you hear me?"

Very slowly because it was a tremendous effort, he turned his head and found himself looking to two very large, worried eyes.

"You are better .. very much better .. and you have no .. temperature. Is there .. anything I can get .. you?"

It took a long time to understand what she was saying, but at last with an effort he managed to reply:

"I – am – thirsty."

"I will bring you something cool."

He felt her lift his head very gently and once again, because he seemed to remember it happening before, he felt a glass against his lips and thought what he was drinking had a sweet taste, but was not unpleasant.

Then as the mist that had seemed to fill his head began to move away a little he realised it was night and the room was in darkness except for the candles burning by the bedside.

"Where – am – I?" he asked.

"In Paris," Miranda replied, "and you are quite safe and no one shall hurt you again."

The Earl tried to remember what had happened and why he had been hurt, but it was too much effort. He closed his eyes and heard Miranda say:

"Go to sleep. Everything will be all right in the morning, now that you are better."

Her voice was very soft and musical and as he

slipped back into unconsciousness he was glad she was there.

Miranda came into the room and looked enquiringly at Hicks who was just coming from the bedside.

"How is His Lordship?" she asked.

"Awake, Miss," Hicks replied with a grin, "and very disagreeable!"

Miranda did not say anything but moved eagerly to the side of the bed to look down at the Earl. He was propped up a little further than usual on his pillows and was, as Hicks had said, looking extremely disagreeable.

"You are awake at last!" Miranda exclaimed. "I began to think you would sleep like Rip van Winkle, for twenty years!"

"How long have I been ill, and what happened?" the Earl asked sharply.

"It is a long story, do you think you are well enough to listen to it?"

There was a silence before the Earl replied:

"I remember now! We were going to the Opera and there was a mob – they were making trouble."

"They made enough trouble for you," Miranda said, a little throb in her voice. "A brick struck you on the side of the head and knocked you out, and when you fell you fractured one of your legs."

The Earl was aware that one leg felt as if it had a heavy weight on it and he said angrily:

"How long have I been laid up like this?"

"Quite a long time," Miranda replied, "but, please, you must not agitate yourself or worry. The Doctors are agreed that you must have complete rest and quiet."

"Doctors? What Doctors?"

"There have been a number of them," Miranda answered. "The Doctor who attended you after I managed to get you back sent for two skull specialists, but neither of them really knew what to do, except to wait and hope you would get better naturally."

She felt for a moment that the Earl had not heard her for he had closed his eyes.

Then he opened them to say:

"My head still – hurts."

"Of course it does," Miranda said sympathetically. "The edge of the brick caught you on a very sensitive nerve and the Doctors are glad it did not do worse damage."

"And my leg?"

"That is getting better, but you have to rest."

She spoke in a soft voice, but her anxiety was very obvious.

"Doctors are fools!" the Earl said. "The sooner I get up the better!"

Miranda gave a little cry.

"It is impossible, quite impossible! You must not try to do anything too quickly, because you have been unconscious for a long time."

"A long – time?" the Earl repeated slowly. "How – long?"

Miranda hesitated as if she knew it would upset him, and determinedly as if he was forcing her to obey him he repeated:

"How long?"

"Nearly two weeks!"

The Earl stared at her as if he thought he could not have heard aright.

"Two weeks? It is impossible!"

"You are better and talking quite naturally so there is no need to worry about it," Miranda said quickly.

"Two weeks!" the Earl repeated.

Now he remembered that he was in Paris, the war had begun, and Lord Granville not having received any letters from him would be wondering what had occurred.

"I must get better," he said, "and find out what is happening."

As he spoke he felt a wave of fatigue sweep over him and although he tried to prevent it, he found his eyelids were drooping and he knew that although he had no wish to, he was falling asleep.

*

"Are you telling me seriously that the Emperor is a prisoner in Germany?" the Earl asked.

Miranda nodded

"I am afraid so. He capitulated to Moltke with a hundred and four thousand soldiers at Sedan and was taken by the Germans to Schloss Wilhelmshohe which had once been the seat of his Uncle Jerome."

"What happened after that?" the Earl asked.

"I was told by your Doctor that the Empress flew into a terrible Spanish rage when she heard of the capitulation, and in the streets the people were either weeping or making menacing sounds of fury."

"You did not go out?" the Earl asked sharply.

"No, of course not, but Hicks told me that in the Boulevards they were shouting 'Down with the Empire!' just as they were shouting it outside the Opera House the night you were hurt."

"What has happened since?"

"It is difficult to understand what exactly," Miranda

answered, "but there is, I understand, a new Republic. At first the Empress would not believe in its existence, and although she was begged by her advisors to leave Paris, she stayed at the Tuileries, which seems very brave."

It struck the Earl that she was doubtless remembering the humiliation in which Louis XVIII had left, forgetting even his slippers, and how poor old Louis-Philippe with his wife Amelie, had scuttled out of these same Tuileries in an open coach taking only fifteen francs with him.

"The Doctors tell me," Miranda was saying, "that the Empress only got worried when the servants all began to desert her, flinging off their uniforms and stealing everything they could lay their hands on!"

She drew in her breath before she said:

"It must have been terrifying because she could hear the mob yelling outside and finally, the Doctor said, she listened to what the Italian and Austrian Ambassadors were advising her and accompanied by them and her lady-in-waiting left by a side-door and scurried through the galleries of the Louvre."

"I should imagine that was a sensible thing to do," the Earl remarked.

"When they reached the Rue de Rivoli the two Diplomats put the women in a carriage, and they drove to the house of a State Councillor in the Boulevard Haussmann, but he had already gone."

"Do you mean to say they let the Empress go alone?" the Earl asked.

"So your Doctor heard," Miranda replied, "and she found the same situation at the house of her Chamberlain. Eventually in despair, she went to the house of her dentist, Dr. Evans, an American, who is a friend of your Doctor's."

"This is the most amazing muddle I have ever heard!" the Earl murmured. "But go on."

"He was at home, and he smuggled the Empress out of Paris in his own coach, telling the sentries on the barricades that he had with him 'a poor old woman on her way to a lunatic asylum'."

"So she is safe!"

"We hope so. The Doctor was told that Dr. Evans persuaded an Englishman to take the Empress to England, and now the mob have occupied the Tuileries."

The Earl put his hand up to his forehead.

"I cannot believe this has all happened so quickly! It is unbelievable!"

"That is what I keep thinking," Miranda agreed, "and I feel as if Paris and France will never be the same again."

The Earl was certain this was true, but even so the whole thing seemed too fantastic for him to believe it.

His Doctor, however, when he called later in the day, confirmed everything Miranda had told him.

That, and what he had learned from Hicks, made the Earl more determined than ever that he must get up and see things for himself.

What was more, he had to make sure that Miranda was taken to safety.

However, he found to his fury that he had to cope not only with the pain in his head, which at times seemed almost blinding, but also with a fractured leg which he was strictly forbidden by his Doctor and the Surgeon to move until it was healed.

"Stay where you are, My Lord," the Surgeon said. "To go hopping about on crutches with the streets in their present condition would be, if nothing else, risking being crippled for life."

The Earl found himself obliged to obey but he resented every moment that he had to stay in bed and both Hicks and Miranda found him very impatient and disagreeable.

They were, however, relieved when the Earl had a number of callers who arrived to see him once they learned that he was capable of talking to them.

The *Vicomte* had not returned from the country, but almost everybody else seemed to be in Paris, including Blanche d'Antigny.

She had refused to stay in the safety of the Château which Bisch had bought for her, and as soon as she arrived she came to see the Earl.

She looked so beautiful, dressed in an exquisite gown by Frederick Worth, wearing jewellery worth a fortune, and bringing with her the exotic fragrance of a scent which lingered in the room long after she had gone, that she seemed to Miranda to have come from another Planet.

The Earl was obviously delighted to see her, and after Blanche arrived, and Miranda left the bedroom she felt suddenly depressed.

She knew it was because she was comparing herself with the elegant, flamboyant and fascinating woman whom she was sure the Earl must love to distraction.

"How bored he must be with me day after day," she told herself as she sat downstairs in the Salon waiting for Blanche to leave.

Certainly after she had gone the Earl seemed to have cheered up quite considerably, and he said:

"What did you think of my last visitor?"

"She was beautiful," Miranda said in an awed voice, "and I would love to see her on the stage."

The Earl thought that most of the parts that

Blanche played were certainly not suitable for Miranda to see.

He also thought she should not have come in contact at all with a woman who would be looked upon with disgust by their relatives and ignored by them as if she actually did not exist.

He told himself, however, it was impossible for him to chaperon Miranda properly in the present circumstances in Paris.

But he made a note in his mind that before they returned to England he would make sure to tell her not to mention Blanche to any of the rest of the family.

Another caller who brought the Earl all the gossip he wanted to hear and whom he had known in England as a Member of Parliament was Henry Labouchere.

He was a strange, eccentric character. In his lifetime by the time he was thirty-nine, he had filled the roles of lover, cynic, Stage Manager, Diplomat and a radical Member of Parliament.

He had, however, lost his seat at the same time as he inherited £250,000. He promptly bought a quarter share in *'The Daily News'* and appointed himself as Paris Correspondent, which trebled the newspaper's circulation.

He was outspoken, witty and was, the Earl had always been told, irresistible to women.

When he had called, half as a friend, half as a journalist, the Earl had found him so informative and at the same time so amusing that he had begged him to come again.

Henry Labouchere did not need to be pressed.

He found it a relief to be able to talk freely with another Englishman and he also enjoyed the excellent food and wine with which he was provided in the *Vicomte's* house.

He took to arriving at all sorts of different hours, sometimes twice a day, to relay the latest information to the Earl and enjoy his reaction to it.

"You will hardly believe what is happening now," he said as he came into the Earl's bed-room to find him sitting up in bed with every newspaper that Hicks could buy scattered on the silk coverlet in front of him.

"Tell me, what really is happening?" the Earl commanded. "I cannot make head nor tail of the nonsense written in most of these journals."

"I only wish it was nonsense!" Henry Labouchere replied. "But first I must say good-morning to your beautiful nurse. I suppose you realise, My Lord, how lucky you are to have one? With the wounded pouring into Paris, most men in your condition would have no ministering angel by their side."

Miranda laughed at him and the Earl said:

"You are not to turn my Ward's head with your flattery and your compliments! In fact, if you do not behave yourself, I shall have to send her out of the room when you visit me!"

Miranda gave a cry of horror.

"Oh, please," she said, "I do so enjoy hearing what Mr. Labouchere has to tell you. It is so much more exciting to hear the news from him than to read it in the newspapers."

"That is what I think myself," the Earl said, "so tell us, Labouchere, what is happening now."

"As I told you yesterday," Henry Labouchere said sitting down in a comfortable chair by the Earl's bed and accepting with relish a glass of champagne which Hicks automatically brought him as soon as he arrived.

"You will not believe it, but the trains are bringing people into Paris as fast as they take them out."

"What do you mean?" the Earl asked.

"It is obvious that the Germans are advancing, and we are going to find ourselves besieged. Now, despite the fact that the Government has some two hundred and fifty thousand sheep as well as forty thousand oxen in the Bois and even some in the smaller Squares, if the population continues to increase, and the siege lasts long enough, dogs, cats and rats will be terrified!"

Miranda gave a little cry of horror.

"You mean .. we shall be reduced to .. eating them?"

"Undoubtedly, if the Government lets people pour into Paris at the rate they are doing now," Henry Labouchere replied. "I have just been writing an article for my newspaper in England in which I have said that it is likely there will be considerably over two million inhabitants to feed, rather than the one and a half million the Government are counting on now."

"Surely something can be done?" the Earl asked in a tone which Miranda knew meant he wished he himself was in a position to do something.

Henry Labouchere shrugged his shoulders.

"The trouble is that no one has enough authority, and for some extraordinary reason not only are the French determined that they will be safer in Paris than anywhere else in their country, but inquisitive British and Americans are pouring into the City!"

He laughed before he said:

"I have brought to read to you an advertisement inserted by some estate agents which reads:

> "Notice for the benefit of English gentlemen wishing to attend the Siege of Paris: Comfortable apartments, completely shellproof; rooms in the basement for impressionable persons."

He read as he spoke from a newspaper which he held in his hand, then threw it onto the bed in front of the Earl who picked it up with an expression of incredulity.

"The whole thing is mad!" he said. "What I intend to do as soon as I can possibly get out of this damned bed is to take Miranda away and return to England."

"I think you would be wise to do that," Henry Labouchere agreed. "It is not going to be very amusing when the Germans really break through the outer defences and dig in."

"You have said this before," the Earl said crossly, "and, quite frankly, I cannot believe that the French will not make an effort to prevent them from getting as far as Paris."

"They can make an effort," Labouchere agreed, "but it is very doubtful whether it will have any effect. Moreover, spy-mania has swept over the City so that another thing I came to advise you was that on no account should you allow this lovely girl to go outside the door unless she has at least two men with her to protect her."

"Are you suggesting that someone might take me for a German?" Miranda enquired.

"No, but you are not wholly French and all sorts of ridiculous situations have arisen."

He paused before he added:

"One of the first foreigners to be arrested was a young Journalist on *'The Morning Post'* who was suspected of being an *Uhlan* and was very roughly treated before he was released. I would hate anything to happen to anyone as beautiful as you!"

The Earl realised that Labouchere's compliments made Miranda shy.

He told himself she was too young for this sort of thing and the sooner he could get her away the better.

Ignoring the advice of his Doctor, and despite the warnings from both Hicks and Miranda about his condition, he insisted on trying to get onto his feet, only to find himself back in bed.

Not only his leg but also his head hurt him abominably, but he was determined to try again and continued to struggle to his feet, even when there was no one with him.

By dint of his driving determination he managed within a few days to move about the bedroom and only occasionally found himself forced back onto his pillows with a blinding headache.

"Please .. please take more care of .. yourself!" Miranda begged. "You are trying to do too much too quickly and the Doctor told me that it might have a permanently detrimental effect."

"The Doctor is an old woman, and you and Hicks cosset me so much that I think I shall go mad!" the Earl said. "I have to find out what is happening and, what is more, we have to get out of Paris."

"I am sure we shall be quite safe here."

"I am quite certain we shall not!" the Earl retorted. "Anyway, I have no intention of sitting through a siege, which may be very much more unpleasant than anything you or I can imagine!"

There was a little silence, then Miranda said:

"I know you have no time for looking after me, and that you would worry because I am with you. Would it not be best, while there is still time, for me to go away so that you can be here on your own?"

The Earl looked at her to see if she was being sincere and realised that it would be impossible for her to lie to him, or even pretend without his being aware of it.

He had learned from Hicks how devotedly she had nursed him when he was unconscious, and he knew she was very different from the sophisticated and spoilt women with whom he had spent his time in the past.

"Whatever I decide to do," he said aloud, "you are going to do it with me! So, instead of making difficulties, try to think of what we shall need for the journey to the coast, and make sure your things are packed so that when necessary we can leave, as I intended to do before, at a moment's notice."

A few days later, on the 19th September, Labouchere came in the morning to inform the Earl that the British Ambassador, Lord Lyons, and the last of his staff had left Paris.

The Earl was astounded.

"It is a disgrace!" he said. "There are still a great number of British in this City and they had no right to leave it without doing what they can for their own people."

Labouchere was silent for a moment. Then he said:

"The Army of the Meuse under the Crown Prince of Saxony has planned to envelope the North side of Paris, while the Prussian Crown Prince's Third Army is reputed to be swinging round on the Southern side."

The Earl's lips tightened.

"That means that we have to do something and do it quickly!" he said. "The first thing is to get our luggage out."

He smiled as he added:

"I have a feeling that Miranda would be loath to leave behind all the beautiful gowns she now possesses, and I think it a good idea for Hicks to go ahead of us."

"I agree with you on that score," Henry Labouchere said, "but it is not going to be easy. The trains for sometime have refused to take any luggage, and there are scenes of chaos at all the railway stations."

The Earl, however, was determined that they must all get ready to leave.

Having purchased a large and sensible, but Miranda thought, uncomfortable Brake, Hicks, with two strong men to protect him, drove off towards the last gate of Paris which was still open.

It was impossible for the Earl to see him leave, but Henry Labouchere who, in his capacity as a Journalist had a great deal of influence, managed to get him through.

He came back to report that after waiting some hours, bribing the officials who wanted to quibble over his papers, Hicks was in fact, out of Paris and, if he kept to his instructions, on his way to Boulogne where the Earl's yacht would be waiting.

The Earl had written to his secretary in England as soon as he was well enough to do so, to explain that he had been slightly injured in an accident.

He was to inform Lord Granville to that effect, who would then understand why there had been a cessation of communication.

Strangely enough, letters had been coming in and out of Paris more or less regularly, and the Earl had found when he was well enough to read it, a great pile of mail from England.

There were letters from his Solicitors, the managers of his estates, his race-horse trainer, his secretary, and over half-a-dozen envelopes which held the faint scent of gardenias and were addressed with a flourishing, flowery hand-writing which he recognised.

He expected that Irene would write to him. At the same time, he had a great reluctance to open and read what she had written, knowing that she would be begging him to return as soon as possible and reiterating over and over again how much she missed him.

It was, in fact, nearly a week before he forced himself to open the first of her envelopes, and when he had read what it contained he lay back against his pillows conscious that the wound in his head was throbbing from the anger which convulsed his whole body.

Lady Irene had written:

> "I know, dearest Thornton, that you will not mind that I have told Papa how much we mean to each other. He had asked me why I seemed so depressed and I told him it was because you had been obliged to go away and how desperately I missed you.
>
> "Papa was very sympathetic and I know you will want to speak to him as soon as you return, and therefore, I can assure you, he will be ready and willing to have you stay at the Castle."

The Earl was well versed in the wiles of women and knew that Lady Irene was not a particularly intelligent woman. But it seemed she was being unexpectedly shrewd in handling this situation.

She had spoken to her father to make sure that the Earl could not escape easily and, to make him realise, unless he was very obtuse, that he was more or less committed now to propose marriage to her as soon as he returned.

He told himself this was what he ought to have expected.

He had not actually said the words that Lady Irene

was longing to hear and had thought, perhaps foolishly, that she would not dare to assume that there was any real understanding between them until he had done so.

He knew also how eagerly the Duke would welcome a rich son-in-law and that he would very probably speak to other people of his daughter's imminent engagement.

His worst fears were confirmed when he opened the fourth letter which Lady Irene had written to him, and which started with a large number of reproaches because he had not written to her.

> "How can you be so heartless, dearest and most beloved Thornton, as to leave me so apprehensive about what is happening to you when after waiting eagerly day after day for the post to arrive, there is no letter from you?
>
> "Surely you cannot be so busy in Paris that you do not have time to send me just one little line of love?
>
> "If it were possible I would send a carrier pigeon to coo outside your window and remind you that I am waiting and longing for the moment when I see you again.
>
> "Papa keeps asking if I have any idea of the day when you might be expected back in England, and yesterday, when he was at Windsor, he told Her Majesty about us and she was delighted!
>
> "I feel sure she will give us one of those large and quite useless Silver Rose-Bowls which we shall not know what to do with ..."

The Earl could read no further, but flung the letter down on the bed and told himself that, siege or no siege, he would not leave Paris and he would rather die than walk blindly into the trap that Lady Irene had set for him.

He put the letters away and did not of course, mention them to Miranda.

He kept thinking, however, that if she were not with him, and, although he denied it, an encumbrance, he would, as soon as he was well enough, go off to other parts of the world, where Lady Irene would be unable to find him.

He found himself thinking of visiting Africa, Egypt, or even the Far East.

Then he knew that he was being over-dramatic, and somehow he had to extricate himself from the machinations of Irene without having to suffer the indignity of becoming an exile from his own country and his estates.

"Dammit all!" he said fiercely. "It is ridiculous that I should be pressured into marrying anyone I do not wish to marry, and for that matter, have no intention of marrying!"

The more he thought of Irene, the more he told himself she was the last type of woman he would want as a wife at the head of his table and as the mother of his children.

It was one thing to have a fiery and insatiable mistress, but a very different thing to have her permanently with him as the Countess of Kyleston.

If he had never thought of it before, he thought now that to spend his life wondering if every man they met at a party had either been his wife's lover before they were married or likely to become one after, would be a living hell from which he shrank with every nerve of his body.

At the back of his mind the Earl had always envisaged that when he eventually married, it would be to a woman he could put in his mother's place without feeling embarrassed about it.

Although she had died when he was only sixteen, his mother's influence had been so strong that he had not only never forgotten her, but she occupied, although he would not have expressed it that way, a special shrine in his heart, where no other woman had ever encroached.

Perhaps because he had been idealistic as a boy, his mother had always seemed to exemplify everything that was fine, beautiful and dignified in a woman.

He would have felt as if he was deliberately insulting her if he installed in her bedroom at Kyle someone like Irene, whose morals were no better than those of Blanche d'Antigny.

"I will not marry her! Nothing in the world will make me do so!" he told himself defiantly.

And yet as he spoke, he saw as if it suddenly materialised in front of him, the Duke's face, eager for a wealthy and important son-in-law, and Her Majesty the Queen's stern and disapproving glare.

"What can I do?" he asked himself aloud. "What the devil can I do?"

He thought that the letters lying open, with their flowery handwriting and their insidious scent of gardenias, laughed at him because he was so impotent.

CHAPTER FIVE

"*Monsieur* Labouchere, *M'Mselle!*"

As the door opened and Henry Labouchere was announced, Miranda gave a little cry of delight, and jumped to her feet.

"I am so glad you have come," she said, "I was beginning to think you had forgotten us."

"How is His Lordship?" Labouchere asked advancing towards her.

"Asleep," Miranda replied, "he had a restless night, and it was only when I persuaded him to let me massage his forehead that he finally fell asleep and has not moved since."

The way she spoke in her soft, musical voice was tremulous, and made Harry Labouchere look at her sharply before he asked:

"You are not falling in love with him, are you?"

Miranda's eyes widened, then the colour came into her cheeks.

"Of course .. not!"

"It would be a great mistake if you did."

"Why?" Miranda asked in surprise.

Henry Labouchere settled himself comfortably in an armchair and as a servant came into the room with the inevitable glass of champagne he took it from him and waited until he left before he replied:

"You are very young, and have very little knowledge of the world. Let me warn you that the Earl is not for you."

"I am .. aware of .. that," Miranda said, thinking of the beauty of Blanche d'Antigny and how alluring she had looked when she visited the Earl.

"What is more," Henry Labouchere went on, "I think you will find that your Guardian, as he calls himself, will be married soon after he returns to England."

"M..married?" Miranda faltered.

This was something she had never expected, and she could not understand why she felt as if something touched her heart in a way that was extremely painful.

"I have heard since the Earl arrived in Paris that Lady Irene Curtis is telling everybody in England that they are secretly engaged and that her father, the Duke of Cumbria, has already launched out on various projects because he will have a rich son-in-law."

Now Miranda was looking at Henry Labouchere wide-eyed, and at the same time her thin face seemed unusually pale, although he did not appear to notice it.

Instead he said:

"It will of course be a very sensible marriage if Lady Irene ever brings it off. She is an acknowledged beauty and one would have to look far and wide to find anyone as handsome as Kyleston."

Miranda knew that was true, but she had not anticipated that as soon as they arrived in England the Earl might get married.

This meant that she would be left alone immediately with a lot of relatives she had never seen before and who, whatever he might say, would doubtless disapprove of her because her father had married her mother.

Feeling that she could not bear to hear more or even think about it, she rose to her feet and walked to the window to stand looking out into the garden.

"But that was not really what I came to tell you," Henry Labouchere said behind her. "In fact, I am the bearer of bad news."

"Bad news?"

Miranda turned round to him again and asked in a different voice:

"What has happened?"

Labouchere drew in his breath before he said:

"This morning, the two Prussian Armies which, as you are aware were making an encircling movement round Paris, joined hands near Versailles which surrendered without a shot!"

Miranda gave a cry of horror and Labouchere finished:

"The siege is now set. Paris is severed from the rest of France!"

There was silence before she said:

"I cannot bear it! And the Earl will be very upset. If only we could have left yesterday, as we planned."

"I was not aware then that it was your last chance," Henry Labouchere said, "but the light and fast carriage I purchased for you was ready, and so were the two excellent horses which would not have tired easily."

Miranda made a little sound that was almost a sob as he went on:

"It is no use regretting. We cannot put back the clock, and the Earl was not well enough even to drive through the gates of Paris, let alone contemplate the long journey to the coast."

"I know," Miranda agreed, "and it is entirely because he insisted on doing too much too quickly. But he was determined to see to everything himself."

Now it seemed a disaster that the Earl had gone to bed the night before they were due to leave feeling, as he admitted, rather heavy-headed.

Then, as Miranda had found in the morning, he was completely incapacitated by one of the blinding migraines which made it impossible for him even to see or to talk, let alone get out of bed.

The Doctor had come when she went for him and merely said it was what he might have expected if the Earl would not do what he was told, and he must accept the consequences. The only cure was to stay in bed and rest until he was stronger.

"I have told *Monsieur* over and over again," he said to Miranda, "that head injuries are always unpredictable, and the only possible treatment is rest and quiet."

"I know," Miranda agreed, "but the Earl has a very active mind and he cannot bear to be idle. Despite the fact that he had been warned, he insisted upon calling on his friends to say goodbye."

She had the idea that the Earl had very good reason for seeing a large number of distinguished gentlemen who had either been in Ministerial posts before the fall of the last Government or were in important positions under the new one.

It had been too much for him, although neither he nor Miranda had any idea that the encroaching Armies would move so quickly, and that now, as Henry Lebouchere had said, the siege had really begun.

"What will .. happen?" Miranda asked in a frightened voice. "Surely they will not be able to break down the fortifications and invade the City?"

"I think they will bombard us with long-range guns," Henry Labouchere said, "and plan to starve us out."

"Can they .. really do .. that?"

"I am afraid so," he replied, "and I only wish I could have got you and the Earl away before you had to suffer as Paris undoubtedly will."

He looked at her speculatively before he added:

"You know better than most people what starvation means, and the Parisians will not take it lightly."

Miranda drew in her breath, thinking of how terrible it had been to see her mother growing weaker and weaker every day because they could not afford food.

She was also aware without anyone telling her that there would be riots and looting, and it would be very difficult, even with so many troops in the City, to keep order.

Only when Henry Labouchere had gone, having promised to come back later in the day to see the Earl if he was well enough to see him, did Miranda find herself thinking that if they were obliged to stay in Paris, at least she would be with the Earl.

He would not be leaving her immediately for Lady Irene Curtis, whoever she might be.

It was difficult to imagine that any woman could be more beautiful than Blanche d'Antigny, but she understood the difference between a Lady whom the Earl could marry and a Courtesan, whom he could not.

'If we stay here, perhaps he will forget Lady Irene,' she thought, but knew that was merely a childish hope which had no chance of fulfilment.

She accepted Henry Labouchere's warning that when they returned to England the Earl would be married and knew that this would leave her all alone and frightened.

Because even to think of it made her feel she must be near him, she went up to his bedroom where she had left him asleep.

On her instructions there was a man-servant sitting outside the door in case the Earl should need attention.

When he saw Miranda coming down the corridor he rose to his feet.

"I will take over now, Henri," Miranda said, "and thank you for giving me a chance to be off duty."

She smiled as she spoke and the man grinned back.

"It's a pleasure, *M'mselle*," he replied and hurried along the corridor to get back to his own quarters.

Very quietly Miranda went into the Earl's room.

It was dark for the sunblinds were drawn, but the windows were open and a light breeze made the large room cool.

She crept to the bedside and saw that although the

Earl was not moving his eyes were open and he was awake.

"Are you better?" Miranda asked in a voice that was little louder than a whisper.

"My head feels better," the Earl replied slowly, "but I feel – very tired."

"Then you must rest."

"I remember the way you massaged my forehead to send me to sleep," the Earl said. "It was very effective. I think you might have been a witch in a less civilised age."

"I am quite prepared to be a white witch," Miranda replied with a smile, "but I think now you should go back to sleep."

"I am tired of sleeping," the Earl said impatiently. "What has been happening?"

Miranda pondered whether she should tell him the truth with the risk that it would upset him.

Then as if perceptively he knew what she was thinking, he said sharply:

"Something *has* happened, and I wish to know about it!"

Hesitatingly because she was frightened it would upset him Miranda said:

"The Prussian Armies moving to surround Paris have met to complete the circle without any opposition from the French troops."

The Earl stared at her, then asked incredulously:

"Is that true? Do you mean there was no opposition?"

"According to Henry Labouchere, who called here this morning, Versailles surrendered without there being a shot fired."

"I cannot believe it!"

The Earl shut his eyes as if it was too much to bear and Miranda said quickly:

"I did not mean to worry you, but there is nothing you can do about it, and you must get well."

He did not reply, and after a moment she sat down on the side of the bed and reaching out her hand put it on his forehead as she had the night before and started very gently to massage first his temples, then his whole forehead.

It was a very soft movement, and the Earl felt it was hypnotic.

Despite the fact that he wanted to think over what had occurred, he found himself becoming drowsy and gradually slipping away into unconsciousness.

Looking down at him Miranda thought that he was no longer imperious and rather overwhelming as he was usually, but somehow, although she could not explain it, young and vulnerable, and she wanted to protect him.

How she would do so she had no idea, only her instinct told her that he was in danger, not from the German guns, but from something else – something that had worried and perplexed him and perhaps been more truly the reason for his migraine than his moving about too soon and visiting his friends.

"If only I could help him!" she said looking down at the sleeping man who could no longer feel the touch of her fingers.

Then as she looked at him thinking how handsome he was, and at the same time feeling, although it was of course impossible, that she should make him happy, she knew that what she was feeling was love, and that she loved him.

The Earl got up the next day to find that cannon fire

could be heard in the distance and the streets were filled with people anxious for news.

At the same time, the fortifications were being strengthened and improved every hour of the day.

As Miranda had anticipated, there were mobs moving about the City making a nuisance of themselves and insulting everyone who had been of importance in the old Régime.

The Earl learned to his consternation that Blanche d'Antigny had been attacked at the theatre and she could not appear in the Boulevards without being hissed at and threatened.

She had tried to help those who were arranging charity performances in aid of the hospitals. In fact, Blanche in a white apron helped to serve champagne and liqueurs, and sold her kisses at five louis each.

But there were many people in Paris, the Earl learnt, who blamed the national debacle and the tragic inadequacy of the old Régime on the Courtesans who, it was alleged, had drained men of their will-power and moral sense.

"What am I to do, *mon cher*?" Blanche asked pitiably of the Earl. "I asked the new Prefect of Police for protection, but he only told me to give up my horses to be requisitioned and to stop giving dinner-parties which he thought were an insult to the suffering of the people."

There was no advice the Earl could give her, except to obey the Police, and he could understand in a way how the flaunting of their jewellery, their carriages, horses, the extravagance of the way of life had caused envy to fester amongst the poor and the unemployed until now that they had the chance they were only too ready to take their revenge.

"You should have stayed in the country."

He knew as he spoke that such advice might equally have applied to him, that he should have left Paris when he had the chance, and not embroiled himself and Miranda in the miseries of a country that was not their own.

"What can I do now?" he asked, when he returned to Miranda who was waiting for him, and he felt more helpless and more frustrated than he had ever been in the whole of his life.

Three days later on 23rd September Henry Labouchere burst into the Salon late in the afternoon. The Earl had been wondering why they had not seen him for twenty-four hours and what was keeping him away.

He and Miranda were sitting looking at the newspapers that were still being printed, although scantily, and both rose to their feet as Labouchere was announced.

"I wondered what had happened to you," the Earl said holding out his hand.

"There is so much to tell you that I do not know where to begin," Henry Labouchere replied, "and you will hardly believe it when I tell you that your last letters which you tried to get out of Paris just before your accident are now on their way to England!"

"But how? I do not understand!"

"I could hardly believe it myself," Henry Labouchere admitted, "but this morning, early because it had been kept a secret, a balloon called the '*Neptune*' was wafted out of Paris over the heads of the astonished Prussians."

"A balloon? It cannot be possible!" the Earl exclaimed.

"Duruof the pilot carried with him a hundred and twenty-five kilograms of despatches, including your letters, and we have reason to believe because of the height he reached without any difficulty, that he would have landed safely, so the experts say, near Evreux, beyond the enemy's reach."

Henry Labouchere spoke so quickly and so excitedly that the Earl could only say:

"I find this is absolutely astonishing! Tell me more!"

"Immediately the *'Neptune'* had left, four other balloons took off in quick succession with, astonishingly, none of their crew being shot down or otherwise coming to grief."

Henry Labouchere threw out his arms in a theatrical gesture as he added:

"The blockade has been broken and now at least there is a means of communicating with the provinces. The Minister of the Interior – Gembetta – is planning to leave the City by balloon and rouse the provinces against the enemy."

Breathless Henry Labouchere took a glass of champagne which a servant had entered the room to offer him and drained it without a pause.

As the servant refilled it the Earl said:

"If I were not confident that you are telling the truth, Labouchere, I would suspect that your imagination had run away with you. A balloon! Who would have thought it?"

"Their location has been kept a closely guarded secret," Labouchere replied, "and although most of them were in bad repair, including the famous *'Celeste'* which you will remember was used during the Great Exhibition, the others have been patched up, and when I spoke to Gembetta I learned that he and the other Ministers concerned are confident that this is an unexpected way in which Paris can be saved."

The Earl thought privately that this must be an exaggeration, but as Labouchere went on talking he sat silent until there was a pause, when he said:

"What I want you to do, Labouchere, is to make sure, and it does not matter what it costs, that Miranda and I leave Paris by balloon!"

For the next few days Miranda felt as if she was living in a fantasy so unreal that it could only be something she had read in a book or dreamt about at night.

The Earl, whose migraine seemed now to have disappeared completely, was organising and making plans every minute of the day for what would be, he felt, one of the most daring actions he had ever undertaken in his very active and sporting life.

It was only after he had inspected the balloons available, paid a large sum for one, and had to convince a great number of people that he was serious in his determination, that he suddenly remembered that Miranda had a mind of her own.

After dinner when they were alone in the Salon he asked:

"I suppose it is a question I should have put to you before, Miranda, but you will not be afraid to come with me?"

As he spoke he realised it was in fact, a great deal to ask of any woman and something that most of them would undoubtedly refuse with horror.

Paris had learnt that Duruof had landed safely and, as had been anticipated, near Evreux.

What had happened to the other balloons was not

yet clear, and the Earl, while elated by the idea of escape, did not under-estimate the dangers on which he was prepared to embark.

The great bag of highly inflammable coal-gas needed only one stray enemy bullet to turn it into a ball of fire. A favourable wind could change at the last moment to an unfavourable one, which could blow him in the wrong direction and perhaps bring him crashing down on the enemy lines.

He had been so busy learning how to handle a balloon and familiarising himself with the complexities of ropes and rigging, that he had not really considered that while he was prepared to risk his life, he was also risking Miranda's.

Looking at her sitting on the sofa in one of the exquisitely-made gowns he had bought her, he thought that, despite the fact that she was certainly not as emaciated as she had been when he first saw her, she still had a frailty about her.

It made her seem almost ethereal, and at the same time, with her hair arranged in a fashionable style by her new lady's-maid, very lovely.

The thinness of her arms which had not yet filled out very much was concealed beneath a chiffon scarf, making her look like a figure out of a Fragonard picture.

In fact, she did not in the least resemble a sturdy young Amazon, ready to brave the skies and accompany him on what he knew was an extremely precarious flight that might easily end in disaster.

"Listen, Miranda," he said, "if you would rather not come with me, I am sure Labouchere can find somebody with whom you can stay, and with whom you will be perfectly safe."

He paused before he added ruefully:

"Not that anything is really safe, as you well know. On the one hand you face the German shells and starvation and perhaps finally German invaders. On the other we have a fifty-fifty chance of reaching safety, and that perhaps is exaggerating the odds against us."

To his surprise Miranda laughed, and it was a very pretty sound.

"Are you really asking me such a ridiculous question?" she said. "Of course I want to come with you! I am much more afraid of being left alone in Paris than I am of losing my life in the balloon. At least, if I die, Papa and Mama will look after me."

Then as if she felt the Earl would think she was being over-emotional, she said:

"I am quite certain however that we shall reach safety. You have always been successful in everything you have done in the past — why should you fail now? The gods will be on your side."

"I hope you are right," the Earl replied. "I greatly admire your courage, Miranda, and I genuinely should like to take you with me."

She smiled at him. There was no need to speak, for her eyes were very expressive.

"The child is falling in love with me," the Earl told himself uncomfortably. "There is nothing I can do about it now, but as soon as we get to England, I will see she meets a great number of young people of her own age."

When he had gone to bed, however, he found himself thinking how exceptional Miranda was and how different from all other women he had known.

They would have clung to him at the slightest opportunity, wanting to be comforted and re-assured that there was no danger if a horse looked like bolting or if by some mischance the wheel of their carriage was slightly scraped in a near-collision.

'It must be the Kyle blood in her,' the Earl thought and told himself that he would make up later for any discomforts she suffered by seeing that she was properly cared for in the future.

The day came when they drove to the launching-pad, where the balloon had been set up, in the Place St. Pierre in Montmartre, the highest point of Paris.

Now the Earl could not help having distinct qualms about taking Miranda with him.

It had been a great disappointment the previous day when he had learnt from Labouchere that a balloon which was released with despatches for the provinces had disappeared into a thick fog at an altitude of a few hundred feet.

But today there was sunshine, and the Earl was assured that the breeze was not only blowing in the right direction, but strong enough to carry them quickly over the Prussian lines and further on to land where he hoped and prayed they would be safe from being captured.

He had bought with Labouchere's assistance two enormous fur coats, one for himself and one for Miranda.

They were not an expensive fur, for although he had been quite prepared to pay for something good, Labouchere had said sensibly:

"As the weather is still warm, you will not need furs once you land, and these can be thrown away or given to any peasant who has helped you to the ground."

The Earl saw the common sense of this and he said to Miranda:

"I think the best thing we can do is to wear riding-clothes, because if, as I hope, we land in open country, we should be able to buy horses which will carry us far more swiftly than any sort of vehicle which would have to keep to the roads."

Miranda saw the reasoning of this and she put on the very elegant riding-habit he had bought her which was far more suitable for the Bois than for a flight into the sky.

It had a well-fitting jacket and, what was more important, short riding-boots which would at least protect her ankles from the cold.

Labouchere had insisted that they wear fur hats, and Miranda swathed her neck in a chiffon scarf, and they also had thick gloves.

"It is very cold up in the sky," he had told the Earl, "as all those I have talked to about ballooning have told me, and you do not want to escape from starvation only to find yourself down with pneumonia."

The Earl was sensible enough to take all the advice he could get, and in the balloon, besides their very light luggage, which was all it was prudent to carry, they carried bandages and a bottle of brandy.

There was also some food, in case, as Labouchere pointed out, they landed in some isolated spot where there was nobody to offer them any sort of hospitality.

The Earl took with him a large amount of ready money, having fortunately before the siege started, cashed a large cheque at a Paris bank.

But even if he had not done so, Blanche's protector, Bisch, offered to advance him any money he required.

The Earl thought this was less out of kindness than because he was delighted to have him leave Paris and be well out of reach of Blanche.

Blanche however came to bid him a fond farewell, and kissing him passionately said:

"I shall be praying, *mon brave*, every moment that you are in the sky! But I feel that *le bon Dieu* will protect you, and perhaps once all these horrors are over, we shall be together again."

"I sincerely hope you are right," the Earl replied.

He kissed her again, and as he said goodbye he kissed her hand and said:

"Thank you, Blanche, for all the happiness you have given me. Whatever people may think about you, I know you are a good woman."

There was a little pause and Blanche said:

"Because you believe in me, and because I am horrified at the way those who once applauded me now revile me, I have decided to turn part of my house into a hospital."

"A hospital!" the Earl exclaimed.

"I have already arranged for forty wounded Breton soldiers to come in next week. I will care for them at my own expense, and help to nurse them back to health."

The Earl was astonished, but he could only say quietly:

"I was right, Blanche, you *are* a good woman."

He knew as he spoke that it was something he could not have said about the majority of the great Courtesans, but he had always known that Blanche was different.

She insisted on giving a pretty jewelled bracelet to Miranda as a parting gift, and to the Earl a rather gaudy set of cuff-links set with rubies and diamonds which he knew he would never wear.

At the same time he thanked her for them, and only when she had left the house did he say to Miranda:

"You must promise me that you will never tell anybody when we reach England who gave you that bracelet."

Miranda looked at him in surprise, and he explained:

"My relatives and anybody else with whom you come in contact once we leave France, would be very shocked that you even knew the name of Blanche d'Antigny. From this moment therefore, I want you to erase her from your mind, except occasionally you might remember her in your prayers."

"She was very kind."

"You must do as I say," the Earl said firmly and Miranda meekly agreed.

There were plenty of well-wishers to see them off as they climbed into the balloon which Miranda thought was a specially pretty one with a pattern in blue and pink on the huge bag.

The basket had appeared quite large until they were inside it. Then it seemed rather flimsy, especially compared to the teams of men who were to guide the unpredictably bobbing, flimsy elephant into the air so as not to foul the nearby roofs.

At last, after they had said goodbye to Henry Labouchere who kissed Miranda on both cheeks, the order was given to cast off the anchor-ropes and the balloon began to rise, spinning and jigging.

It was then that the crowd which was increasing every moment since they had embarked began to cry:

"*Vive la France!*" "*Bon chance!*" and "*Vive la République!*"

Waving and shouting, their voices began to fade away as the balloon rose higher and higher, and now the Earl could see beneath them the Prussian soldiers staring upwards.

They made no effort to try to shoot them down.

Then, as they drifted into some light clouds and for a moment even Paris itself was out of sight, he turned to Miranda and said, a note of exultation in his voice:

"We have done it! By God, we have done it, Miranda! We have escaped!"

He then helped Miranda to sit down on the soft cushions which lined the bottom of the basket and when the balloon was proceeding in the right direction and not jigging or bobbing so violently as it had been, the Earl joined her.

For a moment they both felt too emotional to speak.

Then Miranda put out her gloved hand and the Earl took it in his, smiling at her from beneath his fur hat.

Clothed in furs she looked like some small animal that had just emerged from a wood.

The experts who had seen them off had told them to wait for at least three hours before starting the descent to the ground.

"Take care not to come down in a wood, *Monsieur*," one of them said solemnly, "and, of course, you must avoid water. If the bag descends on top of you, you might be drowned!"

"Thank you for the warning!" the Earl said with a hint of laughter in his voice.

He had been told and re-told a thousand times in the last few days of every ghastly accident that might befall him.

But he told himself the only thing to do now was to hope for the best and, when the time came, use his common sense.

He had, however, taken care to learn how to estimate exactly how much ballast should be released as they rose and to make sure that he did not deflate the balloon too quickly as they came down so that they crashed rather than glided onto the ground.

He was well aware that the science of ballooning, while it had advanced considerably during the Great Exhibition in 1867, was still in its infancy.

And yet to be a Pioneer in a sport which had never come into his life previously was an excitement, even a pleasure, that he could not conceal.

"I suppose you know, if we do reach England," he said to Miranda, "I will be a hero and you a heroine, who have not only escaped the Siege of Paris, but have entrusted ourselves to a new method of travel which few men and I think only one woman has attempted previously."

"It is very appropriate that you should be one of the first," Miranda said admiringly.

"I can hardly claim that," the Earl smiled, "when I remember De Montgolfier's first 'hot-air' balloon in 1783 was a perilous device in which the passengers had to stoke a fire with straw and wood, immediately beneath the highly inflammable paper envelope!"

He paused before he added:

"It was in fact, so perilous that Louis XVI proposed that the first manned flight should be made by two criminals under sentence of death!"

Miranda chuckled and the Earl went on thinking to himself that two years later Blanchard managed to cross the Challen in a *charliere* having to throw out even his trousers in an effort to maintain altitude.

It seemed extraordinary that as early as 1793 the French were using balloons for military purposes, but had then let all their expertise be forgotten.

The Earl had found in the last few days that all the balloons in Paris had been put away in the Gare d'Orleans factory to rot.

Now it appeared that once again the balloon had come into its own, and he decided that once he reached England, he would see the Army Chiefs of Staff and impress on them that it would be a mistake not to use this very effective way of carrying mail or, as in his case, escaping over the heads of the enemy, without their being able to do very much about it.

The Earl in fact, was making plans for the future which he was sure would give him a new interest and perhaps a new activity that was different from anything he had undertaken before.

Because he was so intent on his thoughts, he was quite surprised when looking at his watch he found they had been travelling for over two hours, and they could soon be considering bringing the balloon down lower so that they could see where they were.

A strong wind had carried them more quickly than was anticipated, and he was sure it would be a great mistake to go too far so that they found themselves immersed in the English Channel rather than on the flat, empty French fields which was what he hoped.

He was aware that Miranda had sat very quiet by his side as if she knew he was thinking and had not interrupted.

Once again he thought she was different from any other woman he had ever met, who would by this time be clinging to him with both hands and insisting that his arms were around them.

They would doubtless be crying with fear, so that he could wipe away their tears and assure them with his kisses that they would be safe.

He smiled at Miranda and as she smiled back, it struck him that wrapped in furs she looked very attractive with her grey eyes that held the unmistakable look which had begun to worry him.

The Earl had had too much experience with women not to know when one had fallen in love with him, and there was no need for words to tell him what Miranda was feeling.

He knew that whatever was happening to them both, she was happy simply because she was with him and he was there.

"I must not make her unhappy," he told himself.

He remembered almost with horror the scenes, the tears and misery he had evoked without meaning to, in so many women.

"Dammit, it is not my fault," he had said often enough.

Again he told himself it was not his fault if Miranda had fallen in love with him, and there was really nothing he could do but hope that she would get over it.

Then, as the hands on his watch told him it was definitely time to take their bearings, he reached up to start deflating the balloon.

CHAPTER SIX

It was over one and a half hours before the Earl, with what he congratulated himself on being extraordinary expertise, guided the balloon down into a large field in which he saw the harvest had already been reaped.

He could have descended far earlier, but he realised from the direction of the wind, the compass, and maps he had brought with him that he was being borne in the direction of Boulogne.

He reasoned sensibly that the nearer he could get to

the place where his yacht was waiting, the easier it would be for him and Miranda to reach it.

One thing was quite obvious from what he could see: there were no hostile Germans in this part of France.

The peasants were working normally in the fields and they stopped to stare in astonishment at the balloon coursing overhead.

The dusty roads were empty of anything more sinister than white cattle drawing farmyard carts.

The Earl found himself excited and intrigued by the way in which he could manipulate the strange, ungainly bag under which they were flying.

At the same time he knew that Miranda had been right, and that the gods had indeed favoured them in that the wind was in the right direction and they had passed over the enemy lines without a shot being fired in their direction.

He took care to avoid the woods as he had been warned, for there were quite a number which would have proved a very uncomfortable, if not dangerous landing-place.

When finally he had let out enough gas to bring them down, he thought with satisfaction that he had actually found a new interest which he had every intention of exploring further in the future.

When they reached the ground there was an unpleasant bump, then as the huge half-empty bag keeled to one side, tipping the basket, the Earl reached out his hand to protect Miranda.

There was no need for him to do so, however, for quite sensibly she was crouching as low as she could in the bottom of the basket and neither of them was hurt in any way when they landed.

Then as the Earl stepped out and extricated himself from the mass of ropes he saw, although the field had appeared from the air to be deserted, people were running from every direction towards them.

There was no doubt that they were excited and completely overwhelmed by this visitor from the sky.

By the time the Earl had lifted Miranda out and onto the ground, there was a crowd of men and women around them and the balloon, all talking at once.

The Earl explained that they had come from Paris and had escaped from the Germans, and he knew as he spoke that they could hardly believe it.

They looked at Miranda and himself as if they were supernatural creatures from another world.

Then galloping across the field on a well-bred horse came a distinguished-looking elderly man who the Earl realised at once must have come from the imposing Château he had seen from the air, the owner of which he suspected owned the field in which he had landed.

The gentleman reined in his horse and introduced himself.

"I am the *Comte* de Villeneuve," he said, "and I believe, although it seems incredible, that you have come from Paris."

"That is true," the Earl replied, "and let me introduce myself: I am the Earl of Kyleston, and this is my relative, *Mademoiselle* Miranda Kyle, whom I rescued at the same time as myself."

The *Comte* was impressed and immediately invited them up to his Château.

He sent one of the peasants to order a carriage to come as quickly as possible and suggested that the Earl and Miranda should walk through the fields to meet it.

The Earl assisted Miranda to take off her fur coat and he had already discarded his own.

He had not been as cold in the air as he had expected, and the sunshine now seemed unexpectedly warm and welcoming.

Looking at Miranda's face, he could see how happy she was that they had arrived without any disaster, and that once again, as she had predicted, he had been victorious.

The carriage did not take long to arrive and the *Comte* having given over his horse to a groom drove back to the Château with them, saying he could not wait to hear the latest news from Paris, and to know if things were as bad as the rumours which had reached them alleged.

"I am afraid, *Monsieur*," the Earl replied, "Paris is in for a long and unpleasant siege. I can only feel extremely grateful that we have been able to escape."

When they reached the Château, which was a handsome building and furnished with taste, there was a number of the *Comte's* relations there.

The Earl found himself having to repeat everything he had already said about the siege, the mood of the people, and their anger over the defeat of the French Army.

Living in the country, the *Comte* dined early, and the Earl and Miranda soon after their arrival were taken upstairs where they found the little luggage they had brought with them in the balloon had already been unpacked.

Miranda could choose only from the two Worth evening-gowns she had included at the last moment, which she should wear for dinner.

She was aware that they were really too elaborate for

the occasion, but she had nothing else, and because they were so beautiful and so expensive she had felt she could not bear to leave them behind.

She had, therefore, risked the Earl's annoyance at her luggage being too heavy to be included in the balloon.

When she was dressed in an exquisite gown of blue silk with touches of tulle, velvet ribbons, and diamanté embroidery, she hoped the Earl would admire her.

What she did not realise, although the Earl quickly did, was that the ladies of the party received her very coolly.

Because Miranda was so innocent of the Social World, she did not understand that the *Comtesse* de Villeneuve, and most of the *Comte's* other guests who were staying at the Château, suspected that Miranda was not a relative, as the Earl had stated, but his mistress.

It was obvious too that the *Comte* thought the same.

He had made it quite clear as soon as they talked of Paris that he had heard of the Earl's successes on the race-course, as well as in the field of *'L'Amour'*.

Because Miranda was so in love it was difficult for her to notice anyone but the Earl, who looked resplendent in his evening-clothes which he had brought with him in the balloon because, like her, he could not bear to leave them behind.

She was so intent on listening to what he was saying that she was quite unaware of the pursed lips, the downcast eyes, and the disapproving expressions on the faces of the elderly ladies who were sitting almost silent around the dinner-table.

Even if they had wanted to speak it would have been difficult, because the *Comte* had so much to ask, and the Earl was quite prepared to give him the fullest information.

When dinner was over Miranda realised that the Earl was in fact looking very tired, and she suspected, although she was sure he would not admit it, that he had not slept well the night before owing to a combination of excitement with an inevitable anxiety.

Miranda, who had not spoken for some time, said unexpectedly to the *Comte*:

"I think, *Monsieur*, if you will not think it rude, I would like to retire early, and I feel too that His Lordship should do the same. He has not been at all well, which is in fact the reason we did not leave Paris earlier, as had been planned, and it would be a great mistake for him to over-tax his strength."

"Of course I understand," the *Comte* agreed.

The Earl rose to his feet in a manner which told Miranda she had been right in thinking he was very tired.

They left the Salon together and the Earl was aware of the stiffness with which the *Comtesse* and the other ladies said good-night, and the way they avoided looking at Miranda when she curtsied gracefully to them.

Upstairs, the two bedrooms they had been allotted, which the Earl suspected were the only ones available owing to the large number of people staying at the Château, were side by side.

In fact there was a communicating door between them which had not been opened, but which the Earl had noticed when he changed for dinner.

He thought now as Miranda said good-night and went to her own room that he would have to make it very clear on his arrival in England what was Miranda's exact position in his life.

"It will be all right once we get home," he told himself confidently. "The French are always scenting an affair and Miranda is far too well-dressed to look like an ordinary relation."

It was however quite obvious that she did not at all realise how she was being defamed, so it was not important.

They were leaving in the morning on two well-bred horses which the *Comte* had promised to lend to them and the Earl hoped to arrive in Boulogne late in the afternoon.

When he got into bed he realised he was in fact exhausted and his head was hurting him.

In the next room Miranda said her prayers, thanking God that they had arrived safely, and as she lay in her comfortable bed she thought how fortunate they were not to have to spend the night in the open, which she was certain would have been very bad for the Earl.

She had known perceptively that he was not only tired when he came upstairs but that his head was hurting.

She was however too wise to ask questions, knowing it annoyed him, for he had asserted over and over again before they left Paris that he was perfectly well and he refused to be mollycoddled any longer.

"Please God, take care of him," she whispered in the dark and knew that she felt protective towards him as she had when he was lying unconscious and had later relied on her, almost like a child.

She must have fallen asleep, then awoke, suddenly alert, as if somebody had called her.

The room however was very quiet, but she was almost sure she had heard somebody speaking next door.

She lit a candle and got out of bed. Then moving silently on bare feet over the soft carpet, went to the communicating door which opened into the Earl's bedroom.

She listened and although everything was silent, she was still apprehensive.

Then so quietly that it would have been impossible for anyone to hear her, she turned the handle of the door and opened it just a crack.

She knew then that the Earl was tossing and turning in the large four-poster bed on the other side of the room.

For a moment she hesitated, then she went back and picking up the candle from beside her bed carried it with her and opened the door.

He was still moving from side to side, but as she reached him she was aware that he was asleep, yet restless as he had been before when his head was hurting.

She put the candle down on the bedside table and sitting on the side of the mattress bent forward to put her hand on his forehead.

As she did so he murmured:

"I have – to get – away! There – must be some – escape!"

She realised he was worrying as he had before as to how they could get away from Paris, and very gently massaging his forehead she said softly:

"We have escaped! We are safe! Go to sleep!"

It was the way she had talked to him before when he was unconscious, and she thought that somehow her voice had reached him without him being aroused.

Then he said more loudly:

"I will – not marry – no Irene – no! no!"

For a moment Miranda's hand was still, then as the Earl turned again as if to move away from his problems, she realised that what she had heard was very significant.

With her fingers still massaging the Earl's forehead, she reasoned it out for herself.

Henry Labouchere had said that Lady Irene Curtis had been telling everybody in England that the Earl would marry her when he returned from France.

But Miranda was sure now that the reason why the Earl had been so strangely preoccupied and obviously worried the last week they had been in Paris was not only because of the difficulty of finding a way for them to escape from the besieged City.

She had not missed the half-dozen letters which had arrived just before the siege started and with their coloured writing-paper and scent of gardenias could only have come from a woman.

She had seen them strewn all over the bed once the Earl had opened them, and he had from that moment been so extremely disagreeable that she had known something had seriously upset him.

She had not at the time connected his mood with the letters which she was sure came from some lady who loved him, and she imagined, because she was jealous, he must love her in return.

When Henry Labouchere told her about Lady Irene, she had been convinced that the letters were from her and supposed that the Earl felt angry and upset because he could not be with her.

Now she knew the explanation was very different, her instinct telling her that the Earl did not wish to marry Lady Irene and was in fact apprehensive as to what he could do about it when he reached England.

Suddenly she felt as if her heart was singing because he did not love the woman who had been described as being so beautiful and such a suitable wife for him.

But she was afraid for the Earl.

Suppose, even though he had no wish to marry Lady Irene, he was forced to do so because she was of such social importance?

"If they are married and he does not love her," Miranda reasoned, "he will be very unhappy."

The idea of it was like a pain in her heart.

He was now lying still, and once again what he had called 'the magic of her fingers' had done its work and had soothed away the pains in his head so that he had fallen into a deep and dreamless sleep.

In the faint light of the candle Miranda thought that, now he was relaxed, he looked very much younger than he did in the daytime. Once again she thought of him as a child; a small boy who needed her help and, strangely enough, her protection.

"I must save him!" she told herself.

But, as she tip-tooed back to her room carrying the candle with her and shut the communicating door very quietly behind her, she had no idea how she could do it.

The next day, having obtained everything they required from the *Comte*, they set off to ride across country, which was far quicker than by road, and the Earl was in high spirits.

He was much better after a good night's sleep, and Miranda was aware of this without having to ask him how he was feeling.

The *Comte* had sent their luggage to Boulogne in a

fast vehicle drawn by two horses which he declared would arrive as soon as, if not before, they did.

Because it left long before breakfast, at which they spent some time over the meal, and Miranda was certain the Earl had every intention of stopping on the way for luncheon, she thought this was possible.

"I think by this time," the *Comte* said as he waved them farewell, "the news of your arrival has reached Boulogne, so be prepared to be welcomed by the Mayor."

"I hope not!" the Earl exclaimed.

Miranda suspected, however, that the *Comte* had already sent a groom ahead very early in the morning to make sure that he had the credit of having been the first person to meet them after the balloon had landed.

As she had anticipated, the Earl wished to stop for luncheon and they found a small town in which there was what appeared to be a comfortable *estaminet*.

They stabled their horses and, when the Earl had ordered the food that could be provided, Miranda found she was hungry and ready to enjoy every mouthful.

They sat in an alcove at a table where there was a window looking out over an unkempt garden at the back.

"We have certainly made this an exciting adventure," the Earl said, "and before we reach Boulogne, I want to tell you Miranda, once again, how splendid you have been! There is not a woman of my acquaintance who would have behaved in such a courageous and uncomplaining manner as you have done."

Miranda flushed at his praise, then as she realised how kindly he was looking at her, she said:

"I have .. something to .. suggest to you .. but I am afraid you might think it .. impertinent."

The Earl looked surprised.

"I cannot believe anything you could say to me would be impertinent, Miranda, and, of course, I am prepared to listen."

He wondered what she was thinking and was aware that she seemed deeply embarrassed.

She looked very attractive with her long eye-lashes dark on her cheeks because she was unable to look up at him.

She had not worn her riding-hat in the balloon but the fur hood which Labouchere had insisted upon and which was now with their coats in the hands of the *Comte* who told them laughingly he would keep them as museum pieces.

Instead Miranda had on her head a very attractive and up-to-date riding-hat that the Parisiennes wore when they showed themselves off in the Bois.

It had a blue gauze veil that fell down the back and Miranda's fair hair glowed like gold beneath the small brim.

"What is worrying you?" the Earl asked.

"I am .. afraid you may be .. angry at what I am .. about to say."

"If it makes you happy, I promise I will not be angry."

Not looking at him Miranda said in a low voice:

"Last night .. you were .. talking in your sleep."

"You heard me?"

"I came into your .. room," she said hesitatingly, "because I heard you tossing and thought you might be .. running a fever .. again."

"Why should you think ..?" the Earl began, then stopped. "Go on!"

"You were talking about escaping," Miranda

continued, "then quite clearly you said you did .. not wish to m.marry .. Lady Irene."

Her voice as she spoke was almost inaudible and her cheeks were no longer flushed but very pale, as if she was afraid that the Earl might rage at her.

Instead, after a moment's startled surprise at what she had said, he answered:

"I suppose there is no point in my pretending – to you at any rate. I have no wish to marry anybody!"

"That is .. what I thought," Miranda said, "but perhaps .. as things may be very difficult for you, when you reach England .. I have a suggestion to make."

The Earl raised his eye-brows, but he did not interrupt and she went on:

"I think that some people .. especially your relations will .. be .. shocked that I have travelled with you without a .. Chaperon."

She hesitated for a moment, then she said:

"If it would help you and .. please .. this is only a suggestion .. perhaps you could say that to .. save my .. reputation you have asked me to .. marry you and I have, of course, accepted .."

She spoke hesitatingly and because she felt the Earl might misunderstand, she added quickly before he could make any reply:

"It would only be .. a pretence .. but it might save you from having to .. marry anybody you had no .. wish to make your wife .. and afterwards .. as soon as you are safe .. we could, of course, say that we have .. changed our minds .. and you will be free."

There was a silence as Miranda finished speaking, as if the Earl was stunned and finding it impossible to know what to reply.

Then as he thought of the disapproving faces of the ladies in the *Comte's* household, he realised as he had not done before, that of course when Miranda was staying with him she should have been chaperoned.

Because owing to the unique situation in Paris there had been nowhere he could take her except to the *Vicomte's* house, it had never entered his mind that this emaciated girl, whom he thought of as a child, should have been protected from a man like himself, with a reputation, as he well knew, for 'being a devil with the women'.

When he had been injured she had nursed him and there was no chance of their taking any part in social events or in fact, meeting any of the respectable ladies of Paris.

He had never given a thought to Miranda's reputation and the risk that a very different construction could be put on their relationship from what it actually was.

What astounded him was that she should have grasped what he was feeling about Lady Irene.

Now he suspected that Labouchere had talked to her about Irene and had warned her that Irene was expecting to marry him as soon as he returned to England.

Suddenly there flashed a brilliant light at the end of a very dark tunnel, and he knew that Miranda had found the solution to everything that had been bedevilling him, ever since he had read Irene's letters.

Of course, he argued to himself, he would be expected to offer any woman in the same circumstances the chance to redeem her reputation in the eyes of the Social World, who would not believe for a moment that she had spent so long a time with him without being seduced.

For the moment he found himself almost laughing at the idea that for the first time in his life he was being hung, if that was the right word, for a crime he had not committed.

Yet he knew that amazingly, incredibly, Miranda had found a solution to the dilemma in which he had found himself, and from which he, with all his brains had been able to find no chance of escape.

He realised that Miranda was waiting very nervously for his reply, and stretching out, he said:

"Give me your hand, Miranda!"

Instinctively she put her fingers into his palm and he knew she was trembling.

"There is something I want to say to you," he said, "I want to start by saying once again that I think you are a very unusual and exceptional person."

She looked at him apprehensively and he said with a smile:

"You rescued me from the mob, and now you are saving me from what I feel would be far worse than the Siege of Paris - a miserably unhappy marriage."

"Can I ... do that?"

"I think you can," the Earl replied. "But before I accept what I think is a brilliant idea of yours and one for which I shall bless you for the rest of my life, I want to make sure that it will not hurt you or make you unhappy in any way."

Miranda did not answer, and his fingers tightened on hers as he said:

"I think you will understand that when a man like myself finishes a love-affair, he always hopes it will end without reproaches, recriminations, or anyone being unhappy."

He sighed.

"Unfortunately things do not always work out that way, and sometimes in the past I have been aware that when what the French call *'une affaire de coeur'* is over, it has left the lady in question in tears."

"I can .. understand .. that," Miranda murmured.

"It is something I have never intended," the Earl went on, "in fact, it has always distressed me. So now what I could not bear would be to hurt you irrevocably, Miranda, or to feel that I had, because of your very generous offer, spoilt your life or, as women always say, 'broken your heart'."

The Earl spoke very seriously, and Miranda raising her eyes to his said:

"I want to help you, and if I can be with you for a little .. longer than you .. intended when we reach England, it will be .. something I swear I will never .. regret."

"You are sure of that?"

"I am sure!" Miranda said firmly.

"Then may I say," the Earl replied, "that I accept your suggestion, Miranda, with the deepest gratitude, and at the same time I am much ashamed that I did not think until now, although I should have done, that you should have had a Chaperon."

Miranda laughed and because it was so unexpected the Earl looked at her in surprise.

"I feel that might have been difficult to arrange in Paris," she said. "Mr Labouchere told me that all the ladies who had Châteaux in the country left as soon as they heard that the French were defeated, and I do not think perhaps that *Mademoiselle* Blanche d'Antigny would have been a very acceptable Chaperon!"

The Earl laughed as if he could not help it.

"Now you are frightening me, Miranda!" he said. "If

you talk like that when you reach England, you will deeply shock all my relatives, and they will not think you are a proper person to be my wife!"

"I will be very, very careful," Miranda promised, "but you will ... take me with you to your home?"

The Earl realised as she spoke that she had been worrying in case he disposed of her before he returned to Kyle and he answered:

"As my fiancée, which you now are, you will be everywhere I am. We will go to Kyle as soon as we arrive and I will arrange at once for one of my elderly female relations to come to act as Chaperon. I will at the same time make it quite clear what your position is in my life."

He was thinking quickly that with his genius for organisation once his relatives had accepted Miranda's and his supposed engagement, it would be very difficult for Irene to claim, as she intended, that they were secretly engaged and he must therefore marry her.

"Miranda has saved me," he told himself, "and not only must I make sure that she never regrets it, but I will give her everything in the world that she could possibly want."

As after luncheon they rode on to Boulogne, he felt a great burden had been lifted from his shoulders, his head felt clear, and there was no question of anxiety bringing on another migraine.

As the *Comte* had anticipated, there was not only the Mayor of Boulogne waiting for them as they entered the City, but a huge crowd of people who cheered them wildly.

There were a great number of speeches, champagne

was opened for the Mayor and the Aldermen to toast the hero and heroine of the hour, and the Earl was given the key of the City.

He was then offered accommodation and a banquet whenever he should return to Boulogne.

He thanked them warmly for all they had done, but it was almost dark when at last they were free to board the yacht which was waiting for them in the harbour.

It was a new acquisition of the Earl's, very modern and up-to-date, and in Miranda's eyes very large.

She was in fact, tired because although the time seemed to have passed swiftly because she was with the Earl, it had in fact, been a long and strenuous ride.

She had also been tense and worried as to whether he would think her solution to his problem an intrusion on his private affairs.

That he had accepted the idea made her so happy that it was only when she was alone in her cabin that she wondered how she could bear to leave the Earl when the time came.

She knew that, although it would break her heart, she must never let him be aware of it.

"I love him .. I love him!" she said in the darkness. "He is everything a man should be .. strong, magnificent, and very clever, at the same time kind and understanding."

She could look back now and think how kind he had been when she first approached him, and though he had no idea who she really was, had lent her the money she needed for her mother's operation without asking anything in return.

She had grown up a great deal since she had lived with the Earl at the *Vicomte's* house, and talked to a man as worldly and sophisticated as Henry Labouchere.

There were also the other men who had called to see the Earl and to enquire after him when he was unconscious, and who visited him when he was better.

They had complimented her and even flirted with her in a way that she had never encountered before, and which had opened up new horizons before her eyes which she had not known existed.

She was determined to accept that, while she loved the Earl, she could never mean any more to him than a friend to whom he had given a helping and protective hand.

She would have to be very careful not to cling to him or become a nuisance, as she had learnt from Hicks so many other women had done.

The Earl had been right in thinking that she had heard something about his reputation from Henry Labouchere, but she had learnt a great deal from his valet also.

"If you asks me," Hicks had said in his funny way, "you're the only woman His Lordship's ever known as would look after him like a mother, so to speak, and not been whining and moaning for him to pay her attention."

"I can't imagine many ladies in England doing that," Miranda had said.

"You can't begin to imagine what they're like!" Hicks had said darkly. "Clingin' on to him like poison ivy, they are! Wanting him because he's so handsome, but also putting their hands into his pocket because he's so rich."

Miranda knew she should not encourage Hicks to speak in this way, but she found it impossible not to wish to know more about the Earl who at the moment was incapable of speaking for himself.

She also knew that Hicks, because he loved his master, wished, just in his own way, to protect him as she wanted to, from the women he thought imposed upon him.

"That is something I would never do!" Miranda told herself. "And he must never, never know that I love him!"

The Earl had gone to bed in his cabin thinking that while he was more grateful to Miranda than he could possibly express in words, he was at the same time aware that his conscience was pricking him.

He told himself that if he was truthful, he was behaving badly, and taking advantage of a young and innocent girl who had no idea what she was doing.

But what was the alternative? To marry Irene who was waiting like a hungry tigress to pounce on him the moment he set foot in England?

"I have escaped!" he told himself defiantly. "And I swear that Miranda shall never regret it!"

He had, however, no idea how he could prevent her from doing so, and as he fell asleep he could see her eyes looking at him with an expression that he had seen so often before in women's eyes, and which could only mean one thing – that she loved him.

At the same time, where Miranda was concerned, it seemed different.

It was something he could not put into words – he just knew that her love for him was not the hungry, possessive demanding emotion that women like Irene called love.

It was something very different although he found himself unable to analyse.

'She is indeed an exceptional person!' he thought.

As he fell asleep, it was almost as if Miranda was beside him, protecting him.

CHAPTER SEVEN

The Earl's yacht entered Folkestone harbour early in the morning and his first glance at the Quay told him they were in for a large and noisy reception.

He had not, however, anticipated that as well as crowds of people there would be flags and bunting, and even a Brass Band blaring out a welcome.

He realised, however, that the news must have been carried across to Folkestone from Boulogne during the night.

Meanwhile his Captain had taken the yacht to a

small harbour down the coast where they could spend the night peacefully before making a very early start on the crossing the next morning.

Anyway, he thought ruefully, there was nothing Miranda or he could do about it but accept with dignity and polite gratitude the congratulations that were to be heaped upon them.

Miranda wore one of her prettiest gowns and an attractive bonnet trimmed with flowers, and as she and the Earl walked down the gang-plank the cheers broke out, flags were waved, and they were escorted to a platform on which the Mayor was waiting.

Resplendent in his robes and gold chain, he expressed his congratulations to the Earl not only on his remarkable feat in escaping from Paris, but also for bringing to the notice of the public a skilful but hazardous activity which had almost lapsed.

It was fifty years since there had been balloons flying in England at the time of the coronation of George IV.

To Miranda it was all very exciting, especially when the Earl replied to the Mayor with a witty speech which made everybody laugh, and ended by saying:

"I would like you, as you have been so kind and generous in your welcome to me and to my relative Miss Miranda Kyle, to be the first to offer us your good wishes for our future happiness. Miss Kyle has honoured me by saying that she will be my wife, and I know that she will grace the position. Together we hope to pass on some of our happiness to many other people like yourselves."

This produced an even louder burst of cheers than there had been before, and as they stepped down from the platform, the women in the crowd pressed forward to give Miranda a flower, or merely to touch her, as they said 'for good luck!'

They departed in the carriage which was waiting for them and which, drawn by four of the Earl's fastest horses, had been sent to Folkestone at the same time as he had ordered his yacht to proceed to Boulogne.

As soon as they had driven away and there was no more need to wave in answer to the cheers, the Earl sat back comfortably on the padded seat and took off his hat.

"Thank God that is over!" he remarked.

"They were very kind," Miranda said, "and I suppose all England will be thrilled by the way you have escaped from the siege."

"I think they will account it even more remarkable that I was accompanied by a young woman," the Earl replied.

"I cannot help worrying about how much Paris will suffer if the siege lasts for a long time," Miranda said in her soft voice, "and I wish Mr. Labouchere could have come with us."

The Earl looked at her sharply.

"You have not lost your heart to Henry Labouchere, have you?" he enquired. "He is noted as a lady-killer."

"No, of course not!" Miranda replied, her cheeks blushing pink.

The Earl knew the answer was that she could never love anybody else, because she was in love with him.

He told himself, however, that she had seen very few men, and he would make it his business to give parties and to fill the house with attractive young men in the hope that when the time came to end their pretended engagement, she could easily fall in love with another man.

He was aware, however, as they drove on that although Miranda did none of the things which another woman in her position would have done, such as taking his hand, holding onto his arm, or making an attempt to lay her head against his shoulder, she was vividly conscious of him.

He could feel her vibrating towards him, which made it impossible to ignore her.

Actually, he had no wish to do so as they had so many things to talk about, and when they stopped for luncheon at a large and popular Posting House, they talked animatedly all through the meal, which was edible but in no way to be compared with the excellent food they had enjoyed in France.

They arrived at Kyle at five o'clock in the evening after a rather long and exhausting drive.

They had, however, changed horses twice on the way, which meant they had arrived even sooner than the Earl had dared to anticipate.

As they drove up the drive and Miranda saw the magnificent mansion, which had been built in the 1750s spread out in front of her, she gave a gasp of sheer amazement.

"Papa always said that Kyle was magnificent," she exclaimed, "but I did not expect it to be so big, in fact, exactly the sort of house .. you should .. own."

The Earl understood what she meant by that, but thought he should treat her statement lightly and merely remarked:

"I am glad it pleases you, and now you have the ordeal of meeting the members of the family who, up until now, had no idea you even existed."

"M.members of the .. family?" Miranda faltered, "but .. I had hoped we would be .. alone."

"That is extremely unlikely," the Earl said dryly, "because once I had sent for my yacht, they must have been expecting my return. Also, you must remember, you have to be chaperoned."

"Yes .. of course," Miranda agreed quietly.

But he knew she was disappointed.

There were in fact, nearly a dozen Kyles to greet them, the most important being the Earl's maternal grandmother the Duchess of Manston, who was known to be so formidable that the younger generation quailed when she even looked at them.

To the Earl's surprise, she was immediately very charming to Miranda, telling her she had always loved her father and thought him one of the best-looking of her numerous relatives by marriage.

There were also two of the Earl's aunts with their husbands, his sister and a number of her family, who he thought with satisfaction were exactly the right age for Miranda.

One of his nephews, Alistair, a very good-looking young man of twenty-two, who was on leave from his Regiment, was obviously overcome by Miranda's appearance and, constituting himself her informant and guide, was constantly by her side.

In fact, everybody was so pleasant that by the time they had finished dinner, Miranda's eyes were shining, and she looked so happy that the Earl found himself watching her and listening to her laughter in a way he had never done before.

Now for the moment there was nothing to make them talk seriously, or to be apprehensive as to what might happen on the morrow.

It was still quite early when the Duchess said:

"I think after all your excitements that Miranda should go to bed early, and she has been telling me, Thornton, how badly injured you were in Paris. It must have over-taxed your strength to undertake such a strenuous enterprise so soon after suffering so severe a concussion."

"I am perfectly all right now!" the Earl said aggressively.

But the Duchess said firmly:

"Nevertheless, I see no point in any of us staying up late."

Miranda thought with amusement that the younger members of the party would have much preferred to do so, but were too frightened to say anything.

Carrying their candles in silver holders which a footman lit in the hall, they went up the Grand Staircase, the Duchess leading the way with Miranda beside her.

When they reached Miranda's bedroom the Duchess followed her in and said:

"I want to tell you, dear child, how happy I am that you and my grandson are to be married. You are exactly the wife I would wish him to have, for I have always been afraid he might marry one of those hard, sophisticated London women with whom, up to now, he has spent far too much of his time."

Because Miranda felt guilty about deceiving the Duchess she managed to say shyly:

"I .. I hope I shall make him .. h.happy."

"I am sure you will!" the Duchess replied.

Having kissed her goodnight, she left her with the maid who was to help her undress.

Miranda slept peacefully and the next morning hurried down to breakfast, afraid of missing the Earl should he go out early, and also anxious to see everything she could of the house.

The Earl was already in the breakfast-room with several of the younger members of the family, including Alistair.

The gentlemen rose to their feet when Miranda appeared.

"Good-morning!" she said. "I hope I am not late!"

"There is no fixed time for breakfast in this house," the Earl replied, "and I hope, my dear, that you slept well and dreamt of me."

"Of course I did!"

For a moment Miranda's heart gave a little leap at the way he spoke to her, then she remembered that he was only putting on an act for the benefit of his relatives.

Blushing shyly she sat down at the breakfast-table.

The Earl announced that he was going to take Miranda first on a short tour of the house, then they were going riding as he had many things on the estate he wanted her to see.

"May I come with you?" Alistair asked.

"If you wish to," the Earl replied. "At the same time, you may feel slightly *de trop*!"

"That is exactly what he will be," one of his sisters said, "but I do not suppose it will stop him, if he wants to go with you."

They laughed and teased Alistair because it was quite obvious that he wanted to be with Miranda.

The Earl thought with a twinkle in his eyes that she had certainly made a very quick conquest, and one which might prove useful in the future.

He was, however, too experienced with women not to realise that Miranda was disappointed and wanted to be alone with him.

He told himself he must not allow her to fall more in love than she was already, and he therefore not only agreed to Alistair accompanying them, but suggested to all the other young people that they could come too.

They refused however, and after Miranda had been

shown the main State Rooms in the house which were very impressive, she hurried upstairs to change into her riding-habit.

The horses were already waiting outside the front door, and there was so much to see, so much to admire.

At the same time, she was conscious all the time that it seemed as if the day was especially golden and filled with sunshine because the Earl was with her.

It did not worry her that Alistair was there too; it was enough to know that she could look at the man she loved, listen to his deep voice, and know that what they had been through together had forged a bond between them which she would never be able to forget.

They rode again after luncheon and it was only when they were coming back to the house in time for tea that the Earl suddenly grew tense and uttered an exclamation beneath his breath.

Miranda looked at him in surprise, then saw in front of the house with its long flight of steps and fine Ionic stone columns there was a travelling-carriage.

One look at the Earl's face was enough to tell her without words who it was who had arrived at Kyle, and it was not difficult to guess the reason.

When they had returned for luncheon they had found the newspapers laid on a stool in front of the fireplace in the Library where they all gathered.

"I see there is a long account of your arrival yesterday at Folkestone," the Duchess had said. "I am quite certain that one of the first people who will want to see you and hear of your adventures in detail will be Her Majesty."

"I hope not!" the Earl replied, "I have no wish to

trek to Windsor at the moment, when I want to be here at Kyle."

The Duchess smiled knowingly.

"A Royal Summons will undoubtedly arrive within the next forty-eight hours," she said prophetically.

The Earl groaned and at the same time remembered there had been reporters at Folkestone when they were being congratulated by the Mayor.

They had reported his speech more or less accurately, and described Miranda's beauty in glowing terms.

They had also taken it upon themselves to say that because she was a relative, the Earl had known her for many years, and their engagement had doubtless not come as a surprise to the members of the Kyle family.

The Earl, when he read what had been written, had handed the newspaper to Miranda with a twinkle in his eyes.

After she had seen it and similar reports in the other newspapers, she knew there could now be no possibility of Lady Irene Curtis expecting the Earl to marry her.

And yet now she was quite certain that the owner of the carriage outside the door was waiting inside and was the woman of whom she had been so jealous because she had thought the Earl loved her.

The Earl dismounted and as a groom took his horse he lifted Miranda down from hers.

She looked up at him a question in her eyes, and he said quietly:

"Do not be afraid, and you know how grateful I am that you are with me."

She told herself that was all that mattered, and she was saving the Earl from a marriage in which he would have been unhappy because he had no wish for any wife, whoever she might be.

At the same time, she was quite sure that what lay ahead was going to be uncomfortable and embarrassing.

She longed to hold onto the Earl and for him to reassure her that she was doing the right thing.

But there was no time for him to say anything more, for as they reached the hall the butler came forward to say:

"Lady Irene Curtis, M'Lord, and the Duke of Cumbria are in the Blue Drawing-Room."

"Thank you, Thompson," the Earl replied. "Are they alone?"

"Yes, M'Lord."

The Earl thought with relief that at least there was going to be no audience to overhear what was said.

Without being told Miranda walked beside him, and aware that she was nervous he put his hand on her shoulder to reassure her.

The footman opened the door and they entered the Blue Drawing-Room and Miranda saw at the far end of it the most beautiful woman she had ever seen in her life.

She felt a flutter of fear in case when the Earl saw Lady Irene he would change his mind and wish after all to marry her.

But he walked forward to greet his guests without appearing to be anything but delighted that they had called to see him.

"My dear Irene!" he exclaimed. "What a surprise! Darling, it is delightful to see you, and I hope you have been offered a glass of wine."

He shook the Duke by the hand before he said:

"First, before I begin to tell you of the excitements of my escape from Paris, I must introduce you to my fiancée, a relation, Miss Miranda Kyle, who was with me in Paris."

Lady Irene gave a little shriek.

"So it is true what the newspapers say! I thought when I read them there must be some mistake!"

"Mistake?" the Earl enquired as if he had no idea what she was talking about.

"Thornton, how could you do this to me?" Lady Irene enquired. "You know when you left for Paris you intended on your return to speak to Papa. Until today, he has been waiting to hear from you."

"That is true," the Duke agreed heavily before the Earl could speak. "I understood from Irene that there was a secret understanding between you, and I can only say I would have given your betrothal my unequivocal blessing."

There was a silence after he had finished speaking. Then the Earl said to Miranda in an unemotional voice:

"I think, dear, you would like to change your riding-clothes before tea. Will you tell Thompson before you go upstairs that we will have tea in the Gainsborough Room?"

"Yes .. of course," Miranda replied. "I will .. try not to be too .. long in changing."

"We will wait until you join us," the Earl said, "and I shall want you to pour out the tea."

He walked across the room as he spoke to open the door for her, and as she went out she managed to give him a little smile, and he smiled back.

Then he shut the door and walking towards Lady Irene, who seemed to be frozen where she stood, he said sharply:

"Really, Irene, I should have thought you would have had the good sense not to speak of the situation that existed between us in front of Miranda!"

"Then you admit that a situation did exist?"

"I am not denying it," the Earl replied, "but I think you must either be very obtuse or else unaware of the facts, which are quite simply that I was forced, because a balloon will not hold more than two people, to bring Miranda, who is a cousin of mine, away from Paris without a Chaperon. We stopped for a night on the way to Boulogne and crossed the Channel alone in my yacht."

As he finished speaking, the Earl glanced at the Duke and said:

"At least, you, Your Grace, in these circumstances, could only expect me to behave like a gentleman?"

The Duke nodded.

"I had not realised you were alone together for such a long time," he said in an embarrassed tone.

Lady Irene gave a scream.

"Are you really saying, Papa, that you countenance Thornton's behaviour in jilting me, for that is what it amounts to."

"As I have just explained," the Earl said in a bored voice, "I had no alternative. Miranda is only eighteen, and no one knows better than you, Irene, what her reputation would be in the Social World, to which she is entitled as her father's daughter and my cousin, if I had not offered her the only possible redress for her soiled reputation."

"How can you have been so foolish, so utterly heartless, as to let people be aware that you had been alone together?" Lady Irene stormed. "Surely you could have crept back to England quietly, rather than have that ridiculous ceremony at Folkestone, which was bound to be reported in the newspapers?"

"It was not of my choosing," the Earl replied. 'It all started after our balloon came down in the grounds of the *Comte* de Villeneuve's Château. He lent us horses which we rode to Boulogne, and sent his servants ahead with our luggage."

He made a gesture with his hands as he said:

"They talked, and who is to blame them? Like most people in that part of the country, they had never seen a balloon before, and as you can imagine, everyone in Boulogne wanted to hear what was happening in the Siege of Paris."

"I can understand it was a difficult situation for you," the Duke said slowly.

The Earl realised that while the Duke was outwardly sympathetic, he was trying desperately, because he wanted a rich son-in-law, to think of some way by which he could arrange the marriage of his daughter which he had expected.

The Earl took Irene's hand in his and raised it to his lips.

"I can only express my deepest regrets that this has occurred," he said, "and I beg you, out of the kindness of your heart, to forgive me."

For a moment she seemed bemused by what he was saying.

Then her eyes, which had softened for a moment, became hard and she snatched her hand from his as she said:

"Forgive you, Thornton? I shall never forgive you! I was obviously mistaken in believing that you loved me."

The Earl forced what he hoped was an expression of regret to his face, as he said:

"Circumstances have been against us, Irene, and perhaps one day you will come to think that Fate knew best. After all, I am afraid I shall make a very bad husband."

"That is undoubtedly true!" Lady Irene snapped. "But I loved you, Thornton, and I gave you my heart!"

She made a sound of exasperation before she turned to her father to say:

"What is the use, Papa? We may as well leave instead of harrowing ourselves farther with the idea of what might have been."

"I agree with you," the Duke replied. "Goodbye, Kyle. I cannot help thinking that if you had been a little more astute you might have avoided what is undoubtedly a very uncomfortable and cruel situation as far as Irene is concerned."

"That is the right word!" Irene agreed. "Cruel and heartless! That after all is your reputation, Thornton, towards a number of other women and now towards me also. Well, you have certainly lived up to it this time. I only hope your marriage will be as unhappy as you have made me!"

She seemed almost to spit the words at him before she swept away towards the door, looking amazingly beautiful.

At the same time, the Earl knew that if she could have struck him dead, she would have done so.

He followed her and the Duke into the hall, saw them into their carriage, then walked back feeling as if he had fought a hard battle against what had seemed superior odds, and yet had been victorious.

"I have won! I have won!" he told himself with delight.

Then he remembered that Irene was not the only casualty, there was Miranda also.

He went into the Gainsborough Room which was where his mother had always had afternoon tea.

The tea had already been laid, but there was no one there and he moved to the window to look out into the garden.

The sun was shining on the brilliant colours of the dahlias and the first chrysanthemums.

The green lawn with trees in the background was a scene of peace and quiet, and of a very English beauty.

He found himself thinking about the violence of the mobs roaming the streets of Paris, who would be growing more offensive and more unpleasant as food became shorter and the German bombardment grew more intense.

"How can I have been so fortunate as to get away?" he asked himself. "And also to escape, entirely thanks to Miranda, from Irene?"

He wondered now how he could have faced marriage with anyone whose beauty was only on the surface, while underneath being as dangerous as a prowling wolf and as venomous as an adder.

Then he thought of Miranda and the door opened and she came in.

She was looking, he thought, rather frightened, and yet, in a white gown that could only have come from Paris, very attractive. She seemed to fit into the Gainsborough Room as if she had stepped down from one of the pictures.

She stood just inside the door looking around her in surprise.

"Have they .. gone?" she asked.

The Earl held out his hand.

"Thanks to you, they have gone!"

He saw a light come into her eyes and a radiance to

her face and with a little cry of delight she ran impetuously towards him.

"I am so .. glad!" she cried. "I was so afraid .. so terribly afraid that they might .. persuade you to .. change your .. mind."

As if she had no idea what she was doing, she flung herself against him and as she raised her face to his the words seemed to spill over themselves in her excitement.

The Earl instinctively put his arms around her, and because her joy was infectious and anyway that was what he was feeling himself, without thinking, without considering that he might be making things worse, he bent his head and his lips found hers.

For a moment Miranda's whole body stiffened as if with shock.

Then under the pressure of the Earl's lips she felt her love pour out towards him and his kiss was the most marvellous, the most wonderful thing that had ever happened to her.

Because her lips were so soft and gentle as they surrendered themselves to his, and because he could feel her body quivering with the wonder of what she was feeling, the Earl was suddenly aware that the sensations she was arousing in him were something he had never expected.

They were actually so different from anything he had felt before that for the moment he could hardly believe they were real.

He knew that Miranda was feeling as if he was giving her Heaven and that the love he had seen in her eyes was pulsating towards him as her heart beat frantically.

Her whole body seemed to be diffused with light which for her was part of the Divine and came from God Himself.

He was not certain how he knew such things, but they were there vividly in his mind and as he kissed her and went on kissing her, he found himself enraptured and enthralled by the softness of her and the fact that everything about her made her so different from any woman he had ever kissed before.

Vaguely at the back of his mind he began to realise that what he was feeling for Miranda was something spiritual, something which seemed to be part of what he felt for Kyle.

Then he knew that she was part of this room which always had been his mother's and although he could hardly express it to himself, he knew also that she was the wife his mother would have chosen for him and whom he himself had always sought for and thought he would never find.

The reason why he had sworn he would never marry was that he could not contemplate for a moment putting a woman like Irene or any of the other sophisticated beauties to whom he made love in his mother's place.

Nor could he imagine them, even in his wildest dreams, as the mother of his children.

Now, as he held Miranda against him, as he felt her vibrate with the love she had already given him and also with the rapture his kiss had evoked in her, he knew that this was what he had always been looking for.

This was what had dwelt, although he would never have admitted it to himself, in a secret shrine within his heart.

Only when he raised his head did Miranda look up at him and he thought it would be impossible for any woman to look more radiant or happier in an unearthly manner, as if the sun and all the stars were centred in her face.

For a moment she stared at him, then with a little murmur that was more expressive than words, she hid her face against his shoulder.

His arms tightened as he said, and he thought to himself that his voice sounded a little unsteady:

"Tell me what you are feeling."

"I .. I think I must have .. died," she answered, "and I am in .. Heaven."

"That is what I hoped you felt," the Earl said, "and I think, darling, the explanation is quite simple – you love me!"

There was a little pause before Miranda said in a very small voice:

"I love you .. of course I love you .. but I did not .. want you to know it."

"I have known it for a long time," the Earl replied. "At the same time, I did not realise until now how much I love you!"

Miranda was very still, then she said in a voice that trembled:

"Did .. did you say you .. love me?"

"I love you!" the Earl said firmly. "I have been so foolish, so very, very stupid Miranda, but I did not understand while you looked after me in Paris and during these last days when we have been together, that I was falling in love with you, but in a very different sense from the way I have used that much-abused word in the past."

She moved a little closer to him and he knew she was frightened that she had misunderstood what he was saying.

After a moment she asked:

"You .. cannot really mean you .. love me?"

"I love you," the Earl repeated, "and I know now, Miranda, that there is no reason for us to have a merely pretended engagement. We are going to be married very shortly. You are going to look after me and help me and prevent me from doing any more of the stupid things I have done in the past."

He felt Miranda give a little gasp of surprise, and he knew he was being honest with himself in deploring that he had wasted so much time with women like Irene.

He had the strange feeling that Miranda would change the whole course of his life in the future.

He hoped it would now be worthwhile and a contribution not only to his own reputation but the family of which he was the head, and the country itself.

He could hardly believe he was not imagining all this, and yet it was so vivid, so clear in his mind that he knew it was the truth.

Very gently he put his finger under Miranda's chin and turned her face up to his.

"What have you done to me, my precious, to make me feel like this?" he asked. "How can you be so different from anyone I have known before?"

"I .. I know I am .. dreaming .. I know I am dreaming!" Miranda said, "but .. please .. go on saying such .. wonderful things to me .. just in case I .. wake up!"

The Earl gave a laugh and it was a very tender sound.

"I think I am dreaming too, and I keep asking myself how I could be so fortunate as to find somebody so brave and, at the same time, so adorable, so lovely, who will inspire me as no one else has ever done."

To his surprise he saw the tears come into Miranda's eyes.

"What have I said to upset you?" he asked.

"It is .. because I am .. so happy," she whispered. "I have been so .. frightened of being alone .. after Mama died .. and although I .. tried to enjoy every minute of being with you .. I kept thinking how terrifying it would be when you .. no longer needed me .. and I would have to .. go away and .. make a life of my own .. without you."

She gave a little sob as she said:

"I knew then .. that I would want to .. d.die!"

"My darling, my sweet," the Earl said, "those things will never happen! You will be with me and stay with me and be my wife, and I am absolutely convinced that we shall be divinely happy together and although the world may be astonished, I shall prove to be a model husband!"

Miranda gave a little chuckle and he thought it was the most adorable sound he had ever heard.

"I want you .. just as you .. are," she said. "Every night when I have gone to bed I have thought that no man could be so wonderful and, above everything else, so kind."

She drew in her breath before she went on:

"You were kind to me when I came to you, though you had no idea who I really was, and I realise now how extraordinary it must have seemed to you that I asked you to help me to do anything so .. wrong and so .. wicked .. but I was desperate."

"I knew that," the Earl said, "and only because I knew you were trying to save your mother, did I understand that you were being brave enough to even contemplate such an idea."

"But you were kind and understanding," Miranda went on, "and I realise now that another man might have behaved very differently."

The Earl felt her shiver. He knew that was true and said:

"Forget it! I believe, my darling heart, that God has moved in a strange and mysterious way, but He has brought us together, and if you had not been brave enough to come to me, we might never have met. And I might have gone on searching for you aimlessly in all the wrong places!"

"Now you have found me."

"We have found each other," the Earl corrected, "and I know that while you need me, I need you. What could be a more perfect foundation for a marriage which will not only make us happy, but perhaps all those with whom we come in contact?"

Miranda gave a little cry.

"When you said that yesterday in your speech at Folkestone, I thought it could never come true! Although it seems incredible, we must try, and because you are always successful in everything you do, we shall succeed."

Because her voice was so moving and she looked so lovely as she spoke with her eyes glowing with love, which the Earl knew came from her soul, he could only kiss her.

As he drew her closer and his lips became more demanding, more possessive, he knew that, if this was the first time Miranda had been in love, it was also the first time he had known love in all its glory, and what, like her, he could only describe as its purity.

They belonged to each other, he told himself, and with Miranda he had escaped not only from the Siege of Paris and from Irene, but from so many other things which had spoiled and in a way diminished him as a man.

The future, he told himself, would be very different.

As he felt the sensations which had swept Miranda into a special Heaven echoed within himself, he knew that what they had found together was the eternal love.

It would enrich and enlarge their lives from now until Eternity.

BARBARA CARTLAND'S EXPERIENCE ON HEALTH

1930–1932	Studied Herbal Medicine with the famous Mrs. Leyel of Culpeper.
1931–1933	A patient and a student of Dr. Dengler of Baden-Baden. First use of olive oil as an internal treatment of liver complaints, colitis and inflammation of the bowel.
1930–1937	Helped Lady Rhys Williams giving Vitamin B for habitual abortion and malnutrition in the Distressed Areas. Studied the first use of Vitamin E with brood mares and later for barren women.
1935 onwards	Worked with Dr. Pierre Lansel, M.D., first Practitioner in England to give injections of Vit. B and C. Followed his experiments with hormones for rejuvenation and the Nieheims treatment of Cell Therapy. Studied with two eminent Doctors the effect of oil injection on external Haemorrhoids. Studied the nutritional condition in her brother's Parliamentary Constituency, King's Norton Division of Birmingham, where there was malnutrition from unemployment. Practised Yoga exercises and breathing with the only white Yogi in the world. Wrote in a monthly magazine on the subject. Studied nutrition in Montreal and did two lecture tours in lower Canada during which visited a large number of schools and hospitals.
1939–1945	County Cadet Officer for the St. John Ambulance Brigade, Bedfordshire. Arranged First Aid and Home Nursing Lectures and

discussed Nutrition with doctors from overseas.
Only Honorary Member of the Officers' Mess (Doctors and Psychiatrists) of 101 Convalescent Home, the largest Rehabilitation Centre in Great Britain.
Looked after 10,000 RAF and the US Flying Fortresses until the American Red Cross arrived.
Studied nutrition of the troops and the conditions in the Prisoner of War Camps.
As Lady County Welfare Officer of Bedfordshire Voluntary Junior Commander (Captain) A.T.S., dealt with innumerable complaints over food from RAF Camps, Secret Stations and Searchlight Posts and with the health and employment of pregnant mothers from all three Services. Studied conditions in the hospitals treating the women in the Armed Services.

1945 Was introduced in America to the first B-Complex Multi-Vitamin (synthetic) capsule. On return home was closely in touch with the American manufacturers of Vitamins, receiving regular reports, literature and supplies until the Organic Vitamin Company opened at Hemel Hempstead.

1950 Vitamins saved her life. Kept fifty-two farrowing sows on her farm in Hertfordshire and experimented by giving them and the boars Brewers Yeast from a Brewery. For four years held the record production for Great Britain with an average of eleven a litter. Method copied by Sir Harry Haig for Ovaltine. Her prize-winning bull was given Vitamin E injections.

1955 Published: *"Marriage for Moderns"*, *"Be Vivid, Be Vital"*, *"Love, Life and Sex"*, *"Vitamins for Vitality"*, etc.
Began her lectures on Health.
Became a County Councillor of Hertfordshire,

on Education and Health Committees for nine years.
Studied nutrition with regard to school meals. Deeply concerned with the health and conditions of Old People. Was so horrified at the way they were fed in some Homes, and their general treatment, that her daughter then Viscountess Lewisham visited 250 Homes all over Great Britain.
Following her reports and Barbara Cartland's and the tremendous press publicity involved, the Minister for Housing and Local Government (The Rt. Hon. Duncan Sandys, M.P.) instigated an enquiry into the "Housing and Conditions of the Elderly".
Was on the Managerial Committee of several Old People's Homes and a Patron of Cell Barnes, the largest Home for retarded children in Great Britain.
Visited and inspected innumerable hospitals, clinics and Homes for the Elderly and children. Started her fight for better salaries and conditions for Midwives and Nurses, which brought her into close contact with many of the teaching hospitals and Royal College of Midwives.

1958 Was host to Professor Ana Aslan, founder of H3 on her first visit to England at the invitation of 400 doctors. Also tried Acupuncture and the Cryiac Method of holding a slipped rib or disc.

1960 Started to write monthly for *"Here's Health"*. Co-founder of the National Association for Health.
Answered 5,000 letters a year – 10,000 in 1984.
"The Magic of Honey" (1 million copies), doubled the sale of honey in Great Britain and over the world.
Lectured on Health to:
    The Southgate Technical College

	The Queen Elizabeth College of Nutrition The Hertfordshire Police Cadets Two lectures in the Birmingham Town Hall to audiences of 2,500 Frequent lectures to Midwives, Universities, Rotary Clubs, etc.
1964–1978	Given a Civic Reception by the Mayor of Vienna for her work in the Health Movement. Had private discussions on Health, herbs and health foods with: 　　The Ministers of Health and Sciences in Mexico, Japan and India. Professors and Scientists in Mysore working on the development of agriculture in the famine areas near Kerel with the India Ladies Committee and Official on Health in Bombay, New Delhi and Mysore. In touch with the Indian Guild of Service working among orphans, and in the poor areas in India, and saw the conditions among the first three million Pakistanis which moved into Calcutta in 1958. Visited the new refugee areas in Hong Kong, was the first woman to visit (with the police) the Chinese border seeing the conditions of the workers. Visited Nepal and saw the insanitary conditions in Katmandu and the rat-infested refuse in the streets. Discussed the conditions with officials. Visited hospitals, clinics and Old People's Homes in many parts of India, Bangkok, Hong Kong, Singapore, Switzerland, Austria and France. Taken on a special visit with five doctors and scientists to inspect the Vitel Clinic in France. Visited the slums of Delhi, Calcutta, Bombay, Pnomh Penh (Kampuchea), Tai-wan, Singapore, Rio, Harlem (New York), Glasgow,

OTHER BOOKS BY BARBARA CARTLAND

Romantic Novels, over 370, the most recently published being:

Bride to a Brigand
Love Comes West
The Island of Love
Theresa and a Tiger
Love is Heaven
Miracle for a Madonna
A Very Unusual Wife
The Peril and the Prince
Alone and Afraid
Terror for a Teacher
The Devilish Deception

Paradise Found
Love is a Gamble
Victory for Love
Look with Love
Never Forget Love
Safe at Last
Helga in Hiding
Haunted
Crowned With Love
Royal Punishment

The Dream and the Glory (in aid of the St. John Ambulance Brigade)

Autobiographical and Biographical:

The Isthmus Years 1919–1939
The Years of Opportunity 1939–1945
I Search for Rainbows 1945–1976
We Danced All Night 1919–1929
Ronald Cartland (With a Foreword by Sir Winston Churchill)
Polly My Wonderful Mother
I Seek the Miraculous

Historical:

Bewitching Women
The Outrageous Queen (The Story of Queen Christina of Sweden)
The Scandalous Life of King Carol
The Private Life of Elizabeth, Empress of Austria
Josephine, Empress of France
Diane de Poitiers
Metternich – the Passionate Diplomat
The Private Life of Charles II

Sociology:

You in the Home	Etiquette
The Fascinating Forties	The Many Facets of Love
Marriage for Moderns	Sex and the Teenager
Be Vivid, Be Vital	The Book of Charm
Love, Life and Sex	Living Together
Vitamins for Vitality	The Youth Secret
Husbands and Wives	The Magic of Honey
Men are Wonderful	Book of Beauty & Health

Keep Young and Beautiful by Barbara Cartland and Elinor Glynn
You and Your Health

Cookery:

Barbara Cartland's Health Food Cookery Book
Food for Love
Magic of Honey Cookbook
Recipes for Lovers
The Romance of Food

Editor of:

The Common Problem by Ronald Cartland (With a Preface by the Rt. Hon. the Earl of Selborne, P.C.)
Barbara Cartland's Library of Love
Barbara Cartland's Library of Ancient Wisdom
"Written with Love" Passionate love letters selected by Barbara Cartland

Drama:

Blood Money
French Dressing

Philosophy:

Touch the Stars

Radio Operetta:

The Rose and the Violet (Music by Mark Lubbock) performed in 1942.

Radio Plays:

The Caged Bird: An episode in the Life of Elizabeth Empress of Austria. Performed in 1957.

General:

Barbara Cartland's Book of Useless Information, With a Foreword by The Earl Mountbatten of Burma
(In aid of the United World Colleges)
Love and Lovers (Picture Book)
The Light of Love (Prayer Book)
Barbara Cartland's Scrapbook (In aid of the Royal Photographic Museum)
Romantic Royal Marriages
Barbara Cartland's Book of Celebrities
Getting Older, Growing Younger

Verse:

Lines on Life and Love

Music:

An Album of Love Songs sung with the Royal Philharmonic Orchestra

Film:

The Flame is Love

Cartoons:

Barbara Cartland Romances (Book of Cartoons) has recently been published in the U.S.A. and Great Britain and in other parts of the world.

Children's Pop-Up Book:
Princess to the Rescue